GW00792352

Call Yourself a Friend?

Jackie is back to school and exams. But when her friend Bernie is knocked down by a drunken driver her world turns upside down. How can Jackie continue to visit Bernie *and* concentrate on her studies? Meanwhile, boyfriend Kev gets into trouble when he takes the law into his own hands.

Third in the series of books about Jackie and Kev.

The Author

MARILYN TAYLOR is a school librarian who lives in Dublin with her husband and the family cat. When she was a teenager, there was no such thing as books for teenagers. Now, having survived her own adolescence and those of her three grown-up children, she is filling that gap. She believes that books for teenagers should be readable, funny and authentic.

OTHER BOOKS IN THIS SERIES

Could This Be Love? I Wondered
Could I Love a Stranger?

Call Yourself a Friend?

Marilyn Taylor

THE O'BRIEN PRESS
DUBLIN

First published 1996 by The O'Brien Press Ltd.,
20 Victoria Road, Dublin 6, Ireland.
Tel. +353 1 4923333 Fax. +353 1 4922777
e-mail: books@obrien.ie
website: http://www.obrien ie
Reprinted 1997, 1999

ISBN 0-86278-500-6

British Library Cataloguing-in-publication Data
A catalogue reference for this title is available from the British Library

3 4 5 6 7 8 9 10
99 00 01 02 03 04 05

The O'Brien Press receives
assistance from

The Arts Council
An Chomhairle Ealaíon

Typesetting, editing, layout, design: The O'Brien Press Ltd.
Cover separations: C&A Print Services Ltd., Dublin
Printing: Cox & Wyman Ltd., Reading

*For the principal, staff and students
of St Louis High School,
in appreciation of the many years of support
and encouragement for my career
as a librarian and a writer.*

*And as always, my gratitude and thanks to
my husband and all the members of my family –
scattered over three continents – for their enthusiasm
and practical help in the writing of this book.*

The Crash

A screech of brakes, a dull distant thud, the blaring of a car-horn that went on and on ...

I'll never forget the terrible jangle of sounds that changed all our lives on that mild, breezy autumn evening, the last Friday of the summer holidays.

Messing around outside Pizza Paradise, the local café in Rathnure where our crowd hung out, Deirdre, Ruth and I were listing our complaints to each other.

'Honestly, the thought of having to go back to school and listen to Miss Kinsella lecturing us about the Leaving Cert and "settling down to hard work",' said Ruth. 'I can feel that stress pain in the back of my neck already, and term hasn't even started.'

'I hear they may be changing the colour of our school uniform to a sort of tartan,' said my best friend Deirdre, slim and pretty in her bodywarmer and Levi's. But then, she even looked great in our present turquoise uniform, unlike Ruth and me. I had a feeling we'd look even worse in tartan.

We were waiting for Bernie, my boyfriend Kev's sister, who was coming in to meet us from Ballytymon, the corporation estate where they lived.

Ruth was peering into the nearby health food shop. She was big into health, and was an expert on the benefits of every vitamin from A to E. Her current obsession was garlic, which was apparently a cure for every conceivable complaint. She assured us you could take it in odourless capsules, but no-one was very keen.

'I wonder where Bernie is?' said Deirdre.

*   *   *

And then came the horrifying crash, from the crossroads further down. For an instant we all froze. The air filled with the smell of scorched rubber. The horn was still blaring in a continuous wail. People were staring in the direction of the noise. Some started running towards the pedestrian crossing.

'Sounds like a really bad crash,' said Ruth, as we followed the crowd. Above the sound of the car-horn we heard a police-siren.

'We'd better go back to Pizza Paradise,' I said to Deirdre. 'We might miss Bernie.'

She didn't reply. Glancing at her, I saw she was standing very still.

'What's wrong?' asked Ruth. Deirdre pointed silently.

Amid the noise and the hurrying people, a small fair-haired figure was sitting on the kerb, crying. It was Sharon, Bernie and Kev's youngest sister.

A horrible fear clutched me. Why was Sharon on her

own? Where was Bernie? The crash, I thought, surely it couldn't have been ...

We knelt down beside Sharon. Putting my arm round her I asked quietly, 'What's happened, Sharon?'

Her tear-stained face had a dazed expression. 'I don't know,' she whispered. 'We were just crossing the road and then there was a screech, and someone pushed me, I think it was Bernie, and then the horn started–'

Deirdre's eyes met mine. I saw the fear in hers. We looked towards the crossing, where a black car was slewed across the road. I could see the driver slumped over the steering-wheel, rocking back and forth, his head in his hands. The sound of the horn was deafening.

Nearby a small group of people were bent over a still figure lying in the road.

Deirdre was the first to react. 'Ruth, stay here with Sharon,' she ordered. She grabbed my arm and we pushed our way to the front of the crowd.

Everything seemed to stop. The shouting, the sirens, the insistent shriek of the horn. And there was silence.

In a kind of prayer I found myself repeating over and over again, 'Please, please, don't let it be Bernie.'

The Discovery

But it was Bernie.

She lay on the road, her arms and legs awkwardly splayed out, her new denim jacket half pulled off, a black platform shoe lying a few yards away. Torn plastic shopping bags had spilled their contents over the road.

Her face was turned away from us, a red stain seeping slowly through the shining golden hair spread out on the hard grey concrete.

*　　　*　　　*

BERNIE

She threaded her way along Rathnure Road through the busy crowds, gripping her little sister Sharon by the hand. She was going to be late meeting Jackie and the others in Pizza Paradise, but she'd had to call into Quinnsworth to get some messages for her ma. Her ma's nerves were bad again and she'd been forced to go back to St Loman's for treatment. The stuff they gave her ma always made her so tired that she had to go to bed.

It was a shame, her ma had been great recently, especially since Kev came back from Germany. But then there'd been a letter from her dad in England, and that had depressed her ma again, reminding them all of the bad times before he'd gone, and of the woman their dad lived with now.

Sharon was tugging at her hand. 'Look, there's Niamh, she's in my class.' Bernie looked across the road and saw Niamh waving to Sharon, and beyond her, in the distance, Jackie, Ruth and Deirdre waiting for them outside Pizza Paradise. She could see Deirdre, in a fab waist-coat, talking away to the other two.

As the green man flashed and the traffic stopped, Sharon pulled her hand free from Bernie's and headed across the pedestrian crossing. Bernie, close behind her, was laden with shopping, and her new platforms weren't great for fast walking.

Half-way across, out of the corner of her eye, she became aware of a black car speeding towards them.

The lights were red. Surely it was going to stop?

But it didn't even slow down. She felt rising panic. Instinctively she dropped her bags and flung herself forward, hurling Sharon at the last second out of the path of the advancing car. She felt herself fall with tremendous force, heard a crack, a screech of brakes, confused shouting.

The last sound that penetrated before she lost consciousness was a car-horn ...

As we approached, a young garda, kneeling beside Bernie, waved us away. Someone handed him a rug which he began to spread over her.

'She's our friend,' I tried to say, but it was like one of those nightmares when you struggle to scream but nothing comes out.

I could hear poor Sharon sobbing behind us. I hoped Ruth would keep her well away.

As usual, Deirdre took charge. 'Has someone called an ambulance?' she said sharply to the garda. She gestured towards Bernie. 'We're her friends. And her sister needs help.'

There was an immediate reaction. People gave us sympathetic looks. A woman garda took charge of Sharon, taking her hand and talking to her quietly.

'We've got to keep her warm,' said the garda, fixing the rug. 'The ambulance'll be here any minute.'

The woman garda spoke urgently to Deirdre, asking for Bernie's name and address. Another garda wrote down all our names and those of some of the bystanders, who, he said, might be needed as witnesses.

'How badly hurt is she?' I forced out the question.

'She hit her head when she fell,' he said. 'She's concussed, and she may have head injuries.'

I caught vague snatches of talk from the crowd. 'It's a disgrace, these fellas driving with drink taken ... no-one could stop in time at the speed he was going ... such a lovely young girl ...'

The ambulance arrived then, and we stood close together in a shivering silent group, Deirdre and Ruth and I, watching them help Sharon into the back. Then they lifted the motionless figure of Bernie on to a stretcher.

And at that moment I knew that nothing was ever going to be the same again.

The Reality

After the ambulance had gone, the receding sound of the siren seemed to echo a scream struggling inside me to get out.

Ruth muttered angrily to Deirdre and me, 'What about the driver? What's happening to him? Aren't they going to arrest him or something?'

We looked at the black car. The driver was leaning unsteadily against the car door. He looked about my dad's age, short and heavily built, with reddish hair. His freckled face was flushed, and his jaw seemed to be quivering uncontrollably as he spoke to the young garda, who was writing furiously in his notebook. Standing nearby, we could hear odd phrases, 'been driving for thirty years ... she came from nowhere ... come to the station ... blood sample ... statement ... witnesses ...'

None of these words seemed to have any connection with the frighteningly still figure of Bernie lying spread-eagled in the road, with bloodstains in her hair.

I felt a wave of anger. 'Surely they're going to

breathalyse him?'

'They did that while you were with your poor friend,' said a woman beside me, 'Sure, you could smell the drink a mile off.'

A few people were pushing the car to the side of the road. The driver got into the squad car with the gardaí.

'What happens now?' asked Deirdre.

'He'll have to give a blood or urine sample,' said the woman. 'I just hope he has to pay for what he did to the young girl.' And she went off.

Most of the crowd had drifted away. The show was over for them, I thought bitterly, but not for us, and not for Bernie.

*   *   *

Not knowing what to do, we started walking to my house, which was the nearest. None of us said a word.

As my brain slowly started functioning, dreadful thoughts zoomed at me one after the other. Suppose Bernie died? What was going to happen to her poor frail mother who depended on her so much to help with the younger children? And Kev, who'd told me the first time I'd met him that his sister was 'brilliant'? I remembered how amazed I'd been to hear anyone describe a brother or sister that way. I'd always considered my little brother, Philip, an irritating fact of life.

Suddenly I stopped. 'Kev!' I said. 'I've got to find him and tell him what's happened.'

'They said they'd send a garda to the house to tell the family and bring them to the hospital,' said Deirdre.

'I've got to tell Kev before they do,' I said firmly. They both looked at me in surprise. Deirdre was normally the one to say things firmly. But something inside told me that this was an important thing that I absolutely had to do myself, even though I dreaded it.

My relationship with Kev had had its ups and downs. It had survived the threats from Sinead, Kev's ex-girlfriend, who'd done her best to break it up. And it had just about survived my involvement with Daniel who'd come to stay with Deirdre last summer and who I still couldn't get out of my mind.

But despite everything, we were still together, and I wanted it to stay that way. And I cared about Bernie, who had been my friend through thick and thin since we'd first met at the disco in Ballytymon. I knew I owed it to both of them that Kev should hear the news from me rather than a garda, or from his distraught mother.

*   *   *

When we reached my house, the silence told me everyone was out. No FM104 blaring from Philip's room, no news from the TV, no clattering of pots from the kitchen. I remembered that Mum was at Keep Fit, and Dad had taken Gran and Philip to see *A Bug's Life*.

In the kitchen I took three Diet Cokes out of the fridge.

'It's so cold,' mumbled Ruth. I realised I was shivering too, even though it was a mild evening.

'It's shock,' said Deirdre briskly, 'we ought to drink hot

sweet tea.' So the Knights of Malta first aid course her mother had made her do had actually come in useful, I thought, despite all Deirdre's grumbling at the time.

'We've got to tell Therese,' said Ruth, as I busied myself putting on the kettle. 'She's Bernie's best friend.'

We sat at the table drinking the tea in a complete daze. 'It's so hard to think properly,' I said, clutching the comforting mug. 'I've got to figure out how to find Kev.'

'And what are you going to tell him?' said Ruth. 'I mean, we don't know if Bernie–' She stopped.

'Bernie's going to be fine,' Deirdre chimed in quickly, but not quite in her usual confident tone. 'I'll ring my mum. She'll know how to find out where Kev's course would be.'

Mrs Lennon was a local councillor and always knew what to do in a crisis. We drank our tea and listened to Deirdre making phonecalls in commanding tones just like her mother's, until soon she had organised everything.

Leaving a note for my mum, we hurried out. Therese, the other member of our gang, was due to cycle over to Ruth's later, so Ruth went home to wait for her and break the news. Deirdre had arranged to baby-sit for her cousin, so she left too.

And I was going to the Training Centre where Mrs Lennon had sussed out that Kev was supposed to be at a class. We were all going to ring each other later to find out what was happening.

As I shut the front door behind us I reflected how unbelievable it was that something so shattering could happen in such a short time. A couple of hours earlier, the only things on my mind had been the depressing prospect of school and exams, the minor row with Kev about his friend Andy, and how long it was going to take me to save up enough money for a new fleece jacket.

But now, none of these things mattered. All that mattered was Bernie.

The Bad News

Once I'd explained that it was a family emergency, the silver-haired woman in the office couldn't have been kinder. Showing me into a small room, she went off to fetch Kev out of a computer class.

I sat in a straight-backed chair in the stuffy little room, staring at the pink roses on the wall-paper, a sick feeling in the pit of my stomach. I'd felt like this after Dad's heart attack when we'd been waiting for news.

But this was different. Then, everyone had rallied round to give us support. This time Kev and his ma were the ones who were going to need the help and support.

When Kev appeared, wearing the loose black jacket he'd bought in Germany, a lock of his fair hair falling in his eyes as usual, my heart lurched with pleasure at seeing him, and dread at what I had to tell him.

'Jackie,' he said in surprise, 'what's up?'

I couldn't meet his eyes. I dropped my gaze to the worn-looking trainers he always wore. I tried to speak, but instead tears started welling up and sliding down my cheeks.

'What's wrong?'

I raised my eyes to his face. 'It's ... Bernie,' I said. 'She's been in an accident.' He came closer and gripped my arm painfully. 'In Rathnure,' I went on, 'she was ... knocked down by a car.' I swallowed. It wasn't easy to get the words out.

His face was grim. 'Tell me.'

'Sharon was with her. She wasn't hurt. But Bernie– An ambulance took her and Sharon to hospital. They wouldn't let us go with them. The gardaí have gone to tell your ma ...' I forced myself to go on. 'They said Bernie might have head injuries.'

For a brief moment neither of us spoke. Then he said, 'Did you see what happened?'

'No. We just heard it.'

'Did you talk to her? How bad is she?' The questions poured out.

'She was unconscious.' A shudder passed through his body. Then he said, 'My ma'll be at the hospital. I've got to get there.' He paused. 'They did say Bernie'd be all right?' I couldn't answer him.

We stood there together. Kev was rigid as a statue, his face grey. I knew I'd have to take charge.

Leaving him in the room I hurried out, found the woman from the reception, and explained the situation. Nodding understandingly, she grabbed a bunch of car-keys from her desk and said, 'Come on, I'll drive you both to the hospital.'

I went back in and took Kev's hand. It was as cold as ice. 'We're getting a lift,' I told him, and we dashed out into the little battered Fiat, Kev in front and me squeezed into the back beside a child's car-seat.

Only then did my thoughts turn to what lay ahead at the hospital.

The Hospital

'How did it happen?' asked Dad.

We were sitting in the living-room at home later that evening. Usually on Fridays I'd be watching 'Friends', my brother Philip would be complaining that he wanted to play with his Play Station, and Mum would be waiting patiently to watch the video she'd got from Extravision.

But the TV was forgotten as I told them what had happened to Bernie.

'Apparently the driver was drunk,' I said. 'He could barely stand up.'

'That's appalling,' said Dad. 'Who is he? Where's he from?'

'We didn't find out who he was,' I replied. 'We were in such a state of shock at the time. We didn't really think about the driver, just about Bernie.'

'That's understandable,' said Mum sadly. 'Such a sweet girl. Her mother must be in bits.'

'And Kev, how is he coping?' said Dad. 'He's very close to Bernie, isn't he?'

'I think he's in shock too,' I said, thinking of the dazed

look on Kev's face as he went with his mother into the intensive care. 'I don't know how they're going to manage at home. They all depend so much on Bernie.'

'Is she going to die?' asked Philip, sounding unusually subdued, for him.

Mum shot him a look. 'Of course not,' she said quickly.

'A skull fracture is worrying,' said Dad. 'Any other injuries?'

'Her aunt said she has concussion and a broken collar bone, and a lot of bruising.'

Dad closed his eyes for a moment as though he didn't want to hear.

I thought back to the awful scene in the hospital waiting-room when Kev and I had arrived. His mother, Mrs Sinnott, her thin face even more drained and pale than usual, her greying hair wild, was weeping uncontrollably. Kev's aunt Joan, whom I knew from my visits to Kev and Bernie, was trying to console her. When his ma saw Kev, she sobbed even louder, and threw her arms round him. Beside his tall figure she appeared small and vulnerable.

'How is she?' he asked hesitantly.

'We haven't seen her yet,' wept his mother.

'She's still unconscious,' said his aunt Joan. 'She's in the intensive care. They said we can see her soon.' In a lower voice she muttered to Kev, 'She might have a fractured skull. And they're worried about brain damage.'

Over his mother's head Kev's eyes met mine in an anguished look. I wished there was some way I could comfort him. But although Bernie was my friend, and Kev my boyfriend, I still felt a bit of an intruder into this family tragedy.

'Is Sharon okay?' I asked.

'She and the other kids are with neighbours,' said Joan. 'She just had grazed knees, so they didn't keep her in hospital. Of course, she's still very shocked.'

A white-jacketed young woman appeared and came up to Kev's mother. I assumed she was a nurse, but she said gently, 'I'm Dr Murray. You can come and see your daughter now.' She turned to Kev. 'Are you her brother?'

He nodded.

'You come in with your mum,' she said. 'Bernie's on a drip, and we're giving her oxygen to help her breathe.'

Kev cleared his throat. 'Will she come round soon?'

'We hope she'll regain consciousness before too long. It's hard to say.'

'How will she be?' whispered Joan.

The doctor hesitated. 'It's too early to tell. She'll be in a lot of pain from the fractures and the bruising. She's under sedation at the moment.'

The questions about skull fractures and brain damage, that no-one dared to ask, hung in the air.

As they followed the doctor into the intensive care, I whispered to Kev, 'I'd better go. I'll talk to you later.' He nodded, his arm round his still weeping mother.

'Tell Bernie–' But would she be able to hear and understand? 'Tell her I was asking for her,' I choked out, as the door swung to behind them.

The Return

I'd always had mixed feelings about the first day back at school after the long summer holidays. The worst part was the loss of freedom, especially on a bright, breezy morning like this one, with white clouds racing across a soft blue sky. Getting up at the crack of dawn and dressing in that awful uniform was a pain, but at least there was no problem deciding what to wear. And there was the excitement of going into a new class and seeing your friends and hearing all their news and what they'd been up to in the holidays.

But, as Deirdre and I sat in the crowded bus on the Monday after the accident, both our minds buzzed with only one topic.

'My mum rang the hospital,' said Deirdre straightaway. 'They said only the family's allowed to visit. Did you speak to Kev over the weekend?'

'No. They've no phone,' I reminded her, 'and anyway I'm probably the last thing on his mind.' But I'd hoped Kev would've rung to let me know how Bernie was. I wanted him to share the sorrow and trouble with me, instead of becoming distant and hard to reach, his usual response to a crisis, as I'd discovered through past experience.

'Everyone keeps asking me if the driver was drunk,' said Deirdre.

'Well, that woman thought he was,' I reminded her. 'And people said he was speeding.'

'And the way he was leaning on the horn for ages afterwards,' she continued. 'I was telling Mum how he couldn't even stand up straight when he got out of the car.'

I stared out of the grimy bus window. 'I feel so bad that Bernie was on her way to meet us when it happened,' I said. 'If she hadn't had to cross that road–'

'There's no point thinking like that,' said Deirdre firmly. 'It won't help Bernie now.' I knew she was right. But I couldn't get it out of my mind.

The bus stopped and more people climbed on, including Ruth.

'It's back to school with a vengeance,' grumbled Deirdre, as we squeezed up to let Ruth, flushed and panting, in beside us. 'I just couldn't get up this morning,' she complained immediately. 'I have this pain in my knee. I'm sure it's stress because of Bernie's accident.'

Deirdre and I exchanged resigned glances. Our strategy, when Ruth started the moan about her mostly imaginary ailments, was to be as discouraging as possible.

'Oh come on, Ruth,' I said severely. 'Why can't you think about Bernie instead of yourself?'

To my surprise, Deirdre said, 'Maybe it's an allergy.' Ruth nodded eagerly, pleased to be taken seriously for a change. But Deirdre went on, 'It must be school. You're probably allergic to the idea of unaccustomed study.'

Ruth looked indignant. I said quickly, 'Did you hear anything about Bernie, Ruth?'

She hesitated. You could see her hurt pride battling with her urge to pass on her news. 'Therese said she heard that Bernie saved her little sister,' she replied finally. 'Bernie pushed her out of the way, and she was hit instead of Sharon.'

'That's just like Bernie,' I said, remembering how protective she always was towards her younger sisters. 'Is she still unconscious?'

'I think so,' she said gloomily. 'They say she might be in a coma for ages. And when she wakes up she could have serious brain damage.'

We were all silent. What exactly did brain damage mean? It sounded so frightening. Could it mean that Bernie wouldn't recover, that she wouldn't be able to speak or walk? I shivered as we pushed our way down the bus and jumped off.

*　　　　　*　　　　　*

We walked up the road, laden with bags heavy with school-books. Hundreds of uniformed girls were converging on the school gates.

As we joined the throng Ruth said, 'I keep worrying about crossing the road since the accident. I mean, that guy drove straight through a red light.'

'*And* it was a pedestrian crossing,' I added. 'I hope he's sent to prison. Not that it'll help Bernie.'

'My mum says drunk drivers often get let off too lightly,' said Deirdre. 'She thinks they should have to go and visit the people they put in hospital.'

'If they haven't killed them,' I said bitterly. 'Look what that driver's done to Bernie. And we don't even know how she's going to be.' I could feel tears coming to my eyes. Deirdre handed me a man-size tissue out of her pocket. I took it gratefully.

We heard someone calling. Therese rushed up. 'Hey,' she said breathlessly, 'did you hear the driver of the car lives in Rathnure, not far from you lot?'

'What's his name?' asked Deirdre. She seemed a bit put out at not being the one with all the information for once.

'Don't know,' admitted Therese, as we pushed our way through the swing doors and headed for the assembly hall. 'But it said in the local paper that he's a businessman, and he's married with children.'

Angry as I was about the driver, I couldn't help thinking, poor children, to have a father who almost killed a girl.

The Note

I sat on my bed among the jumble of clothes, staring hopelessly at the heap of school-books. It was only the second day back and we already had masses of home-work. But every time I sat down and opened a book, memories of the accident and thoughts about Bernie blanked out everything else.

I'd still heard nothing from Kev, and the bits of news I was getting came from Therese, or from Deirdre's mum, who, as well as being a councillor, was chairperson of the residents' association and heard all the local news. In fact everyone appeared to know more about what was hap-pening than I did.

Rock music was blaring from Philip's room, even though I knew he was downstairs playing 'FIFA '99'. I jumped up and marched into his room to switch it off, ignoring the skull and crossbones on the door, and the signs saying: 'Keep Out: Danger Zone' and 'Man United Rules Here'.

His room was a complete tip. Clothes and shoes were

everywhere, a pair of muddy football boots nestled on the duvet, and huge blow-ups of the Irish football team had been stuck on every bit of wall space, most of them ripped and hanging loose. A trail of empty crisp bags led from the bed to the stereo, which was on full volume. A jar of hair gel was open on the table, and its sickly smell was mixed with that of cheese 'n' onion and the dirty socks strewn over the floor.

Trying not to breathe in, I picked my way over to the stereo, beside which was a towering pile of Smashing Pumpkins tapes, some grubby, well-thumbed comics, a stale cheese sandwich with one bite taken out of it, a browning half-eaten apple and three open cans of Coke.

When I got back to my room it seemed as neat as a doll's house by comparison. I picked up my maths book, but before I could open it I heard Mum calling me. I knew Nana and Gran were coming to supper because it was Dad's birthday. Any diversion was welcome. I didn't feel much like polite conversation, but at least it meant I could leave the homework for a while.

*   *   *

'That was a terrible accident your friend had, Jackie,' said Gran as we sat round the table. 'How is she?'

There was a silence as Mum dished out vegetarian lasagne, her speciality. But I couldn't eat it. I'd found myself getting choked up every time I had to talk about Bernie. I knew Gran meant well, and made myself say, 'She's got concussion.'

Gran shook her head sympathetically. Nana, Mum's

mother, who was often quick to make a sharp remark, put down her fork. 'I suppose it was some young fella in a stolen car,' she asserted. 'They're a menace, those joyriders. They should bring back corporal punishment.'

'There's no discipline these days,' agreed Gran, 'but I don't see how using more violence helps.'

'It wasn't a young fella,' I had found my voice. 'It was a man from Rathnure, a businessman. They say he was drunk.'

Nana looked taken aback. 'A businessman from Rathnure? *Drunk?* Are you sure?'

Dad said, 'Jack Lennon told me that more than half of all road accidents are caused by alcohol.' Dad worked with Deirdre's father, who, like everyone in the Lennon family, was always very well-informed about every conceivable subject, or liked to think they were.

I wished they would stop talking about the accident. All of them, even Mum and Dad, once the initial shock had worn off, just seemed to see it as something that you read in the paper, to be discussed as though Bernie wasn't a real person. I could feel myself getting wound up. Mum went into the kitchen and I followed her, just to escape.

When we came back in with the birthday cake, Philip, who'd been unusually silent, was the centre of attention. 'I don't want to be in the stupid school play,' he was protesting, red in the face.

'Oh Philip, don't say that,' said Gran. 'It's a great opportunity to develop your confidence.' Privately, I thought Philip had way too much confidence. And he'd probably be the kiss of death to the play, whatever it was.

Before I could speak, Nana said in a faraway voice, 'I remember being a flower fairy called Twinkletoes in my school play. I wore a little pink skirt and a pixie hat made of petals. The teacher said I showed real promise.'

I tried to picture Nana, with her stiffly curled grey hair and her sensible lace-up shoes and support tights, as Twinkletoes. Dad gave a snort. Mum shot us all a warning glance.

'What is the play, Philip?' Gran put in quickly.

'*Robin Hood and his Merry Men,*' mumbled Philip.

'Maybe you'll be picked for Robin Hood,' said Mum encouragingly.

'Or Friar Tuck. He'll be the right shape after all the crisps he stuffs himself with,' I said nastily, thinking of the wrappers in his room.

'Even one of the Merry Men could be nice,' said Gran. 'Philip would look lovely in green.'

Philip jumped up. 'No,' he howled, 'I can't be any of those. Teacher said I've to be Maid Marian. She said it's to stop us being chauffeurs or something.'

'You mean chauvinists,' I said, giggling in spite of myself. Mum lit the one candle on the cake. Philip glared at everyone as, fighting back laughter, we sang 'Happy Birthday' to Dad.

'So tell us, Philip,' said Dad, when we'd finished, 'who is going to be Robin Hood?'

'Mary Rose Brennan. She's about a foot taller than me, and she's mouldy-looking.'

'She's *what?*' demanded Mum. Philip crossed his eyes and made a gagging sound.

'All right, don't tell me, I can guess,' Mum said.

'Where does he pick up that language?' asked Nana disapprovingly. 'No-one ever spoke like that in our family.'

'Well, she is mouldy-looking,' repeated Philip. 'And I've got to *kiss* her.'

*   *   *

After supper, Mum, Dad, Gran and Nana sat down to play bridge, and I went out into the still, cool evening to get some fresh air before having another go at my homework. Sitting on the low wall in front of the house I thought back to when I'd sat there with Kev not long after I'd first met him. It seemed like ages ago, even though it was only a few months.

Everything had seemed so simple then. I'd wanted a boyfriend, and I'd found Kev. The difficult things that came later, the scenes with Sinead, Kev's threatening ex-girlfriend, Dad's heart attack, Kev's going to Germany and the arrival of the mysterious Daniel from England, and now poor Bernie's horrific accident all lay in the future.

As I sat there reminiscing, a familiar voice drawled, 'Well, Jackie, still messing around when you should be doing your homework?'

It was Andy the Hunk, as we called him, Kev's friend, and Deidre's on-off boyfriend. As usual, he looked cool, lightly tanned, preening himself in a black T-shirt with Phonics scrawled across it in gold. I eyed his red and white American baseball cap. 'It was given to me by a friend I met when I was working in Germany this summer,' he said, noticing my glance.

'Would that be Monika?' I asked innocently, remembering Kev recounting some of Andy's exploits with an adoring German girl who called him 'Andy the Lips' and thought he was wonderful.

'How d'you know about her?' he asked, his flashy grin fading for a moment.

'Oh, we all know about Monika,' I said airily, 'even Deirdre.'

Andy looked embarrassed, something rare for him. 'I'm going to give Deirdre a call,' he said. 'I'm not long back.'

I thought of nice, reliable Mark, who was devoted to Deirdre, and who was always there when Andy the Hunk let her down. Two-timing seemed to be a habit with Andy, and he'd got up to some other stuff in Germany to do with drugs which I hadn't liked the sound of. 'I wouldn't bother,' I said. 'She's otherwise engaged.' A good line, I thought, must try and use it in an essay.

'Anyway,' I said, 'Do you have any idea how Bernie is?' I figured he might have been talking to Kev.

His expression changed. 'Not too good. Kev's in bits over it. He sent you a note.' He aimed a violent kick at the wall. He was usually so laid-back about everything and everybody that for a moment I wondered if he really cared about Bernie. He handed me the note, and waited while I read it.

> *Jackie*
> *Bernie's still in a coma. It's really bad. The doctor said her friends should come and talk to her, though we don't know if she can hear. Can you &*

Therese come tomorrow after school? She's in the intensive care.
Kev

I felt a peculiar mix of fear for Bernie, relief at having heard from Kev, and encouragement because now there was finally something I could do. 'Tell him I'll be there,' I told Andy. For the first time I gave him a smile, jumped off the wall, and went in to ring Therese.

The Coma

'You can't go in to see your friend. She's in intensive care!' snapped the nurse. 'You shouldn't be here at all.' Dismissing us, she turned back to the chart she was filling out.

I looked at Therese. Now was the time for the assertiveness she was always recommending to the rest of us.

But the chilling silence in the corridor, the powerful antiseptic hospital smell, and the curt nurse in her starched white uniform daunted even Therese.

Eventually I said falteringly, 'Bernie's brother told us the doctor wants her friends to visit her.'

'It's to talk to her, to try and wake her out of the coma,' Therese added more firmly, looking the nurse straight in the eye. The nurse hesitated. So Therese had learned something at the assertiveness class.

I glanced nervously at Therese. Even if we were let in to see her, neither of us was sure what kind of state we would find Bernie in. Deirdre and Ruth's advice hadn't been much help. Ruth had said we should sing Robbie

Williams's latest single because Bernie liked it, and she might respond to music. Deirdre said there was no way Bernie could possibly like Robbie Williams, we should sing something by Boyzone. She added that Bernie might not know us, because she could have amnesia. 'Loss of memory,' she explained, in that superior way that could be so annoying. 'Yeah,' said Ruth, 'I have that every day when I start my homework.'

As we stood in the corridor, Dr Murray, who I recognised from that first day at the hospital, emerged from the intensive care. Noticing us in our school uniforms, she smiled and said, 'You're very good to come, girls. Mr Moran, the neuro-surgeon, suggested Bernie might respond to her friends.'

Despite a disapproving look from the nurse, she herded us into the ward, and over to a curtained cubicle.

*　　　　*　　　　*

A thin figure with dark, grey-streaked hair sat in a chair beside the bed. When she turned around I saw it was Mrs Sinnott, Kev and Bernie's mum, her eyes red and swollen from crying, her face pale. But she made an effort to smile at us, a ghost of the sweet, sad smile I remembered from visits to Ballytymon. She was leaning forward and holding Bernie's left hand in both of hers.

Bernie lay motionless, hooked up to tubes and machines, a drip attached to one arm. Her beautiful fair hair had been shaved off, and there were bandages round her head. Her face was chalk-white, and you could see huge bruises on one side of her face and neck, and down her right arm, which was strapped up. But the worst thing was that one of her eyes was open, staring at us, and the other was closed.

I could feel Therese gripping my arm. I put my hand over my mouth to try and hold back the tears.

'I know all this equipment looks frightening, but it's to help feed and support Bernie until she gains some strength,' said Dr Murray reassuringly. 'She can't see you, and she hasn't spoken yet, but she may be able to hear, so just chat to her like you would normally.'

'Her eyes,' I whispered. 'Why–'

'That's just a reflex,' said the doctor. 'It will sort itself out. Don't let it worry you.'

But it did. It made Bernie seem so strange and different, even more than her shaved head and all the stuff she was hooked up to.

Therese was still holding on to me tightly. I could almost feel her summoning up all her courage. 'Hi, Bernie. It's me, Therese.' Her voice quavered a bit, but at least she'd said something.

I kept telling myself, we're here to help Bernie. Aloud I said, 'Bernie, it's Jackie.' There was a silence. My mind blanked out.

'Er, everyone's asking for you,' Therese carried on valiantly. 'We want you to wake up and get better. It'll be Christmas before too long ...' her voice tailed off. Bernie's mum was crying quietly.

I moved closer to the bed and bent down so I could speak directly into Bernie's ear. Suddenly the words poured out. 'Bernie,' I said urgently, 'it's Jackie. Bernie, we all need you, your mum, and Kev, and the girls, and the gang. It's not the same without you. Even if you can't speak or open your eyes, just move your fingers to show us you're still there.' All our eyes were on Bernie's hand, lying limp in her mother's.

In the tense silence I became aware that someone was standing behind me. Even there, I felt the familiar warm glow and I knew it was Kev. I could feel his breath on the back of my neck. I half turned, and looked directly into his eyes. They had a rare soft look, as though he felt the same glow I felt.

Dr Murray gave an exclamation, and we looked at Bernie. Her mum whispered, 'Her hand. She moved her hand.' And it was true, her fingers were fluttering very slightly. Her mum bent forward. 'Come on, Bernie love, keep trying.'

Bernie's fingers moved again. 'Right,' said Therese. 'That's just a start, Bernie. Next time we come we want to see you doing "Riverdance".' Everyone laughed a bit too loudly, even Mrs Sinnott. The tension had eased. Good for Therese, I thought.

As we followed Dr Murray out I looked back at Bernie. One eye was still open. There seemed a very slight tinge of colour in her face. Or maybe it was wishful thinking.

Mrs Sinnott said softly, 'Thank you, both of you.'

*   *   *

BERNIE

She was floating in a huge empty space, flooded with light. She felt peaceful and happy, with no pain. But there was something she was supposed to do and she couldn't remember what it was. Someone was waiting for her, but she didn't know who or where.

Suspended in the air, she looked down from a huge height. Far below there were tiny figures. She could make out a bed with someone lying on it, surrounded by a group of people. They were all gazing at the person in the bed.

She drifted downwards slowly, peacefully. As the scene came into clearer focus she realised the person in the bed was herself. She thought she recognised some of the people, her mother, some girls, a boy she thought she knew. Why were they so sad?

Some of them were speaking, anxiously, insistently. She didn't know what they were saying. They seemed to be pulling her downwards, away from the light and the peace. She wanted to tell them she was well and happy, floating gently like this. But they were forcing her down, down to the sadness below ...

She was lying flat. She couldn't move. She couldn't see. Breathing hurt. Confused voices came and went. Snatches of words. They wanted her to do something. But she couldn't understand what they wanted. Why didn't they leave her alone? Why couldn't she go on floating peacefully, up into the light?

There was a whirring sound, like a machine. Someone was crying. Then a voice saying 'Bernie'. More voices. Her arms seemed to be held rigid. Someone spoke very distinctly into her ear – she was needed, she must respond, she must speak or move.

She tried to tell them she could hear them. But no sound

came out. She felt a wave of frustration. With all her strength she tried to move her hand.

She couldn't tell if she'd succeeded. The effort had drained her. As she drifted thankfully into unconsciousness she thought she heard snatches of laughter. At least they weren't sad anymore ...

The Threat

Deirdre, Mark and Ruth were waiting for us when we came out of the hospital. They stood open-mouthed as the three of us came down the steps grinning.

'Er, how's Bernie?' asked Deirdre, unusually hesitant.

'What's so funny?' Ruth chimed in, sounding put out. 'We thought you'd be shattered.'

'We are,' said Therese. 'It was shattering. I don't know why we're laughing.'

'I really feel more like crying,' I said.

Deirdre nodded understandingly. 'It's release of tension,' she said. 'They told us about it on the first aid course. You're hysterical.'

'Well, I'm not hysterical,' said Kev. He muttered to me, 'Deirdre's such a know-all.'

There wasn't much I could say. Deirdre *was* a know-all. It could be infuriating, but sometimes it came in useful. And anyway, she was my best friend.

'Well, come on, tell us about Bernie,' said Mark. 'Is she still in a coma?'

As we walked to the bus stop, we related what had happened in the hospital. But at the same time, I reflected that there was no way of explaining how we'd felt, the fear, the anxiety, and the incredible moment of joy when Bernie's fingers moved.

*   *   *

When we got off the bus the others wanted to go to McDonald's. I looked at Kev. 'D'you want to go?'

He shook his head. 'I've got to get back to class.' The laughter was gone now, and his face had a closed-up look.

The others drifted on ahead. 'How's it going at home, with the kids and everything?' I asked Kev.

He looked away. 'We're doing all right,' he muttered. 'The neighbours, and our aunt, they've been great.' He paused. Then he burst out, 'But it's no good without Bernie. The kids are really mixed up. Sharon has nightmares, and she won't go to school. And now my dad's heard about it and he wants to come back from England. He rang Joan.'

Kev hardly ever mentioned his dad but I knew things had been bad at home before he'd left. Bernie had once told me that their dad sometimes lashed out at them and their ma in a drunken rage. When he sobered up he was always full of remorse, but Kev hated him for what he'd done to their mother, and to them all.

'Does your ma know he wants to come back?' I asked. He shook his head grimly.

But his mum and dad must have loved each other once, I thought. After all they'd decided to get married and have children. How could things go so wrong? And when it did, why did the whole family have to get hurt, the kids too? It just wasn't fair.

I reached out for Kev's hand. Both his fists were clenched, the knuckles white.

'Your ma,' I said quietly, 'is she at the hospital with Bernie all the time?'

'Most of the time,' he said. 'When she comes home she's too tired to eat. I can hear her crying every night. She can't sleep, and she's taking so many pills.' He looked desperate. 'I'll get that scumbag who ran Bernie down,' he went on bitterly. 'All this mess is his fault.'

He turned to go. If only I could help him, I thought. If only we could be together, alone, away from everyone. I longed for us to be able to talk about his problems, and what had happened to Bernie, and about us, him and me.

But with school, classes and everything else, there never seemed to be enough time. There were almost always other people around. And on the rare occasions when everything seemed right, Kev could be in one of his silent moods. Or he wanted to kiss rather than talk. I wanted to kiss too. But I also wanted to talk.

Hesitantly I put my hand on his shoulder. He stiffened. But then his expression softened. 'Listen, thanks a million for what you did for Bernie.'

My heart leapt at this acknowledgement. 'Kev,' I whispered, 'I feel so bad about Bernie. Seeing her like that.'

He nodded, his face tight with pain. Clasping my hand he said, 'Will you go and see her again? She's not out of the woods yet.'

'Of course,' I said softly. 'We all will.'

'Thanks. See ya,' he said. I gazed after him as he walked away, but he didn't turn round. And he hadn't said he'd call me.

Something in his hunched shoulders revealed his anger and misery. I was worried by the pent-up violence that I sensed in him. Would he do something stupid or dangerous? Should I go after him? But what could I say? I understood the way he felt.

Sighing, I followed the others into McDonald's.

The Big Mac

'All this stuff's really bad for you,' announced Ruth, as we demolished our burgers and fries.

'Well I see you ate your Big Mac without any problem,' said Deirdre.

'Only because there was nothing vegetarian on the menu,' retorted Ruth.

'Ruth, you can't have it both ways,' said Therese, leaning across for the ketchup. 'You can't just be vegetarian when it suits you. Anyway, you could have had a fish burger.'

Mark started telling us about his dad's new computer. 'We're on the Internet,' he said enthusiastically. Deirdre yawned and started gazing around the restaurant. 'There's a new guy in my class, Greg Gilmartin,' Mark continued, trying to get her attention. 'He's got a computer at home too and we send each other e-mail and surf the Net.'

'Sounds great,' said Deirdre sarcastically. Mark looked crushed.

Deirdre could be really mean sometimes, I thought, as I

tried in vain to think of something to say about computers
that might make Mark feel better.

*　　　*　　　*

There was a commotion from the family at the next table
where two little kids were having a fight. The younger one
had thrown all her Chicken McNuggets on the floor and
was trying to take a bite out of her brother's Big Mac. He let
out a roar and knocked over her strawberry shake.

The distraught mother was trying to mop up the mess.
The father, young and nice-looking in a leather jacket,
seemed vaguely familiar. He smiled apologetically over
towards us, as he tried to pacify the kids. 'Sorry about the
noise,' he said. 'They can be little sods sometimes.' Then
he looked at us more closely, and said to Therese, 'Aren't
you Bernie Sinnott's friend? You live near her, don't you?'

Then I remembered. He was Mr Russell, the teacher
from Bernie's school who'd been at the disco in Ballytymon where we'd first met Bernie and the rest of the crowd,
and eventually, Kev.

Bernie had told us that night how all the girls in her class
thought their teacher was gorgeous, and everyone was
desperate to baby-sit for his kids because they got a lift
home from him. I must remind Bernie about that, I thought
for a split second, before the memory of her present condition hit me like a blow.

Mr Russell came over to us. 'I only heard about Bernie's
accident when I got back to school the other day,' he said,
sounding concerned. 'I gather she has head injuries. How
is she?'

Luckily Therese had paid more attention than I had to the details the doctor had explained to us after we'd left the intensive care. 'The X-rays showed a fractured skull, and concussion, and they're watching her carefully to see if there's some kind of internal bleeding, or a blood-clot,' she told him.

I looked at her admiringly. How could she remember all that stuff? Maybe it's because she watched 'ER'. She'd always said she wanted to be a doctor, but I'd never taken it seriously. Therese went on, 'They won't know if she's got brain damage, or how serious it is, until she wakes up.'

'It doesn't sound good,' said Mr Russell.

'And she's got a broken collar-bone, and cracked ribs,' added Deirdre.

'We've just been with her,' said Therese. 'She moved her fingers. They said that's a good sign. It might mean she's starting to come round.'

Mr Russell looked upset. 'I heard she was knocked down on a pedestrian crossing. I hope they're prosecuting the driver. Is he a local?'

'Yeah, he lives across the road from a friend of my mother's,' announced Deirdre. We all stared at her. 'I only heard that today,' she went on.

'Are you sure it's him?' asked Ruth.

'Yeah,' answered Deirdre, sipping her Coke. 'The neighbour couldn't remember the man's name, he's only moved in recently. But it's definitely him. Apparently everyone on the road knows about it.'

'What did your mum's friend say about him?' asked Therese.

'She said no-one knows anything about him. None of the family talks to the neighbours much.'

'Were you with Bernie when the accident happened?' Mr Russell asked us.

'No, we were waiting for her. We heard it,' said Ruth. 'The gardaí took all our names.'

'Do you remember what the driver looks like?' said Mr Russell. 'You might have to identify him in court.'

Ruth looked anxious. 'I hope we don't have to–' she began.

'I'll never forget that man as long as I live,' I said slowly. I turned to Mr Russell. 'He was short and sort of chunky, with reddish curly hair and a red face covered with freckles. His face kept quivering, and he mopped his forehead all the time as though he was sweating.'

There were surprised looks all round. 'That's very graphic,' said Mr Russell. I was surprised myself. I hadn't realised how clearly that man had lodged in my memory.

*   *   *

Mr Russell got up to go back to his table where his wife was crawling around on the floor picking up the bits of food and other stuff their daughter had thrown down. The kid was now standing on a seat singing the 'Chicken Song' at the top of her voice, wildly waggling her elbows and her behind. All the nearby customers were in fits.

Mr Russell sighed. Raising his voice to be heard above the racket, he said, 'I'll ring the hospital and ask if I can visit Bernie. And I must have a word with her mother too. I know she hasn't been well. She has so much to cope with.'

As he left, I thought how nice it was that he really cared about Bernie and wanted to see her, rather than just saying he was sorry and then switching to another subject, as though what had happened to Bernie wasn't really important. I'd noticed that happening more and more with other people, and it was beginning to bug me.

*   *   *

We trooped out into the evening drizzle and dawdled up the road towards the bus stop. 'I'm knackered,' I said to Mark. 'It's been such a long day, and I've loads of homework to do.'

He didn't answer. That was unlike him, he was usually chatty. His dark hair was damp from the rain and tiny drops spattered his glasses. He took them off and dried them distractedly on the sleeve of his jacket.

'What's wrong, Mark?' I asked, although I thought I knew.

'Well,' he said, after a pause, 'it's the old Andy the Hunk problem.' He grinned wryly. 'He's back from Germany and he's pestering Deirdre again. You know the way she's always had a thing about him.' He sounded anxious. 'He told her I was a nerd.'

So Andy had ignored my advice to leave Deirdre alone. I suspected he hadn't really broken up with the famous Monika from Germany. And Mark was right about Deirdre. Andy was trouble, but gorgeous-looking, with a kind of smarmy charm. None of the rest of us fell for it, but strangely Deirdre, who was usually so sensible and full of good advice, seemed to have a weak spot where Andy was concerned. Though I wasn't going to say that to poor old Mark.

Aloud I said, 'Don't worry, I'm sure Deirdre's had enough of his two-timing by now.'

'Hope you're right,' said Mark uncertainly. I hoped I was too.

The Costume

When I got home I headed for my room and the mountain of homework which had accumulated. Loud voices could be heard from the kitchen and as I tip-toed past, the door burst open and a weird-looking figure appeared.

It was Philip, wearing a sort of skirt made of green tissue paper, and a purple wide-brimmed hat trimmed with a big white rose, which I recognised as having been worn by Mum a few months before for a family wedding. He was roaring. 'I'm not wearing this. No way!'

Mum and Gran were trying to hide their grins.

'There must be some other kind of hat I could wear,' he went on.

'The teacher's note said a hat with flowers,' Mum pointed out.

'It looks very nice,' encouraged Gran. Philip just groaned.

Mum spotted me half-way up the stairs. 'Jackie, have you still got those ballet shoes you once had for dancing classes?' Philip's face turned a deeper red.

'Ballet shoes?' I said vaguely. 'They were thrown out years ago. I've got some old Doc Martens, if they're any use.'

'Doc Martens are going to look peculiar with the green skirt and a flowery hat,' remarked Gran.

'Peculiar?' I said incredulously. 'He looks pretty peculiar to me already, even without the Docs.'

'I keep telling them that,' muttered Philip.

'Come on, Philip, it's just a bit of fun,' Mum said brightly.

'What exactly is the point of it?' asked Gran.

'It's called role reversal,' explained Mum. 'It's supposed to make boys and girls more aware of each other's situations and problems.' Gran nodded, but Philip didn't look at all convinced.

At the top of the stairs, I had a brainwave. I called down. 'What about Nana's pink furry slippers?'

Philip uttered a shriek. 'You must be joking!'

'Thanks for your help, Jackie,' Mum called up with heavy irony.

But at least I'd avoided a repetition of the lecture about how little studying I was doing, which I'd heard several times since school had begun.

*　　　*　　　*

I went back to the hospital each day after school. Although it was never as bad again as the first time, I couldn't get used to Bernie's appearance. Both her eyes were shut normally now, and she occasionally twitched or mumbled something unintelligible.

But after that first day when she moved her hand, there had been no further sign of response. She was still on a respirator, and was hooked up to machines and drips. Dr Murray told us her condition remained critical.

I talked to her about anything I could think of, school, homework, what the gang was up to. But she gave no indication that she could hear me.

The nurse who'd been so sharp with us at the beginning knew me now and was even quite friendly. Mrs Sinnott looked thinner and frailer each day. She would often cry or talk to Bernie in a low tone, or just sit there holding Bernie's hand. But whenever I appeared she made an effort to smile and thank me for coming.

I missed Kev on each visit. His ma told me he dropped in at lunch-times, but had to hurry back to class.

In between talking to Bernie, I chatted to her ma, trying to cheer her up. She told me about the kids, and how lost they all were without Bernie. 'She's the glue that holds our family together,' she said.

I looked at the deep shadows under her reddened eyes, and her faded prettiness, and thought how unfair it was that someone so fragile should have to cope with a husband who'd deserted her, leaving her to live on social welfare with a family of five children. And then for this to happen to Bernie, her main support. It was so unfair.

Each night in bed I tossed and turned, thoughts about Bernie and her family spinning through my mind. By the end of the week I was exhausted. I hadn't had a proper night's sleep since Bernie's accident, and it was beginning to show.

After supper on Friday, having been excused from doing the washing-up, much to Philip's fury, I dragged myself upstairs. When I reached the refuge of my room, I put on Mariah Carey and pulled the *Playboy of the Western World* from my bag. I sat at the desk, staring blindly at the page.

Downstairs I heard a door slam and Philip's complaining voice as he climbed the stairs. Then Mariah Carey was drowned out by the Smashing Pumpkins. When I reached the end of the first scene of the play I realised that I hadn't taken in a word.

I knew it wasn't just the noise. It was everything.

The Long Night

A sharp tap against my bedroom window jerked me awake. Nervously I got out of bed and drew back the curtain. Outside the garden lay still, bathed in silver moonlight. Nothing moved. It must have been my imagination.

But then, as I stood gazing at the garden, I heard a low whistle. Opening the window I leaned out. A dark figure stood in the shadow of the apple tree. I knew immediately it was Kev.

*　　　　*　　　　*

Pulling on a pair of jeans, I crept downstairs and out of the back door, closing it quietly behind me. The night air felt cool and fresh on my skin.

Kev looked dreadful in the strange light, white-faced and grim. He followed me into the garden shed, and we sat side-by-side on an old rug, our backs against the rough wooden wall. For a fleeting moment I remembered sitting like this with Daniel, a long time ago, in the shell house in the park. I pushed away the memory, and the sense of loss that came with it.

Kev was shivering in his thin T-shirt. 'I can't sleep properly since it happened,' he muttered.

'I know,' I said. 'I can't either.'

There was a silence. In spite of everything, I felt a strange excitement at being alone with Kev in the middle of the night. Then he said, 'I had a fight with her you know, that morning.' His voice shook.

'A fight? With Bernie?' She was always so gentle that I couldn't imagine her having a fight with anyone. 'What was it about?'

'It was stupid. She was taking forever in the bathroom, and I was late for class.' He paused, swallowing hard. 'But that was the last time I saw her before ...'

For an awful moment he seemed to be on the verge of tears.

Instinctively I turned and hugged him. He held on to me as though he was drowning, burying his face in my old fleecy pyjama top with blue elephants marching across it. I was filled with mixed emotions. His closeness set up a sort of inward turmoil, a different feeling from when we'd kissed before.

I looked down at his silky fair hair. Could he be crying, I wondered anxiously. And then I thought, why shouldn't he cry when he felt so bad? His ma did, we all did, and sometimes you felt better afterwards. Just because he was a guy, did that mean he wasn't allowed?

We sat like that for a while, and then he lifted his head, and said, 'Sorry,' and rubbed his eyes with his hand. 'It's just that I keep thinking of that morning, and how I was such a shit to her for no reason.'

'Look, it's always like that with brothers and sisters,' I said. 'You should hear me and Philip. But it doesn't mean anything. Bernie probably forgot all about it.'

I knew it wasn't much help. I looked at Kev, and immediately I could see that the moment of closeness was over. His fierce closed-up look was back. But at least he had turned to me for comfort, even briefly, and I had tried to give it.

'It's time the gardaí got that driver,' he burst out. 'They told me he was released on bail after he'd given a blood sample. He shouldn't be allowed to walk the streets.'

'Ruth heard they're interviewing some of the people who saw the accident.' I tried to sound soothing. I understood his anger. But the last thing we needed now was more trouble.

'Well, if they don't get him, I will,' he muttered. 'I know who he is.'

A shiver went through me. I'd found it easier not to think too much about the driver and what he'd done. I didn't want to know his name. I wished that Kev hadn't found it out.

'His name's Gilmartin,' he said. 'Arthur Gilmartin.'

Gilmartin. Where had I heard that name before? Then I remembered. The new guy in Mark's class, the one Mark had told us was a fellow computer buff! Could he be a relation? Unlikely, though if he was, I suspected it wasn't going to help matters. And it might be wiser not to mention the possibility to Kev just now.

Aloud I said, 'Kev, don't do anything stupid. It won't

help Bernie, or your ma. Let the gardaí deal with it.'

He stood up and shrugged. 'I'm not waiting much longer.' He touched my shoulder lightly as he went. The touch seemed to burn into me long after he was gone. So did the menace of his words.

The Rehearsal

Late the next morning I dragged myself down to breakfast. Thank goodness it's Saturday, I thought as I stuck a slice of bread into the toaster and poured myself some orange juice. Everyone else seemed to have had breakfast and disappeared. I knew Dad had gone to play golf with Mr Lennon. I was planning to call round to Deirdre and ask if she'd come with me to visit Bernie.

As I sat munching my toast and marmalade and listening to 'The Best of Strawberry Alarm Clock' on FM104, the front door crashed open and loud voices filled the hall. It sounded like ten people, but when I went to look, it was only Philip and his friend Conor. They marched into the living-room.

'We're having a rehearsal,' Philip announced. 'Make sure no-one interrupts us, Jackie.'

'Who d'you think you are?' I said sourly. 'Liam Neeson?'

He made a face, and slammed the living-room door behind them. I couldn't resist listening. Philip was giving Conor instructions about reading the part of Robin Hood in place of the 'mouldy-looking' girl Philip had complained about.

'And-who-is-this-pretty-maid-I-spy-in-the-green-
-wood?' read Conor in a monotone.

'La sir it is. Eye Maid Marian and why are you?' shrilled Philip, in a high-pitched shriek. 'No, I mean, *who* are you?'

There was dead silence. 'Come on, Conor. What's next?' muttered Philip. I could hear pages rustling. Then Conor obviously thought he'd found the place. 'I-am-the-Sheriff-
-of-Nott-ing-ham–'

'You're not,' spluttered Philip. 'Look, you've turned over two pages. You're s'posed to be Robin, not Sheriff.'

After   a   pause   Conor   intoned,
'I-am-the-famed-Robin-Hood-I-rob-the-rich-to-help-the-
poor-where-may-you-be-going-on-this-fine-morn?'

I could hear Philip clearing his throat. 'Tis May-day sir,' he bellowed. 'And I am. To be. Queen of the May.'

There was another silence. Then Conor said hoarsely, 'And-a-right-pretty-Queen-you-will-be-kisses-her-cheek-
and-leaps-on-his-horse.'

'No! no!' shouted Philip, beside himself with fury. 'You're not s'posed to say that bit.'

More rustling. Then Conor said loudly, 'I'm pissed off with this. Anyway, teacher said you were to rehearse it with Mary Rose.'

'Ugh, gross,' said Philip. 'Let's have a game of FIFA '99.'

Giggling to myself, I scooted upstairs to get my denim jacket. It was nice to be able to laugh at something, even if it was only Philip.

'You must be psychic. I was just going to phone you,' said

Deirdre as she opened the door. Fiacla, the Lennons' cat, darted out and rubbed herself round my ankles. I bent down to stroke her, and she licked my hand, and then gave me a bite with her sharp pointed teeth. Deirdre grinned apologetically as I snatched my hand away.

'I'm always warning you about her,' she said. 'You should know by now why she's called Fiacla.'

Deirdre's mum appeared, holding a briefcase and talking into a mobile phone. She gave me a smile and a wave as she walked past us and got into her car, still talking.

'It's since she's been on the local council,' said Deirdre. 'Mum never gets off the phone. She even brings it into the bathroom.'

'Is she going to a meeting?' I asked. 'On Saturday morning?'

'Yeah,' said Deirdre as we ran upstairs to her room. 'She's meeting some residents about their sewage.'

'Sounds fun,' I said.

Deirdre swept some clothes off a chair for me. She looked great as usual, even in her old jeans and a check shirt, her dark curly hair in a soft cloud round her face.

'You'll never guess who's shown up again,' she announced.

'I suppose it's Andy,' I said discouragingly. 'Surely you're not going to see *him* any more?'

She looked uncomfortable. 'He called round with a present he brought me from Germany.' She showed me a long black silky scarf. It looked expensive.

'Deirdre,' I said, 'You know Andy was close to getting into all kinds of trouble with drug pushers and that kind of stuff when he was there. You'd be mad to get involved with him again.'

She looked stubborn. 'I'm not getting involved,' she said. 'We're just friends.' It didn't sound convincing. She took a bottle of nail varnish from the crowded dressing-table.

'What about Mark?' I asked. 'He's not always going to be waiting around every time Andy dumps you.' I was beginning to sound more and more like the problem page in *Teen Dreams* magazine, usually Deirdre's role. 'Anyway,' I said, 'I've heard some news about the driver.'

Deirdre looked up from painting her nails a glittering dark blue. 'Are they going to charge him with drunken driving?'

'I hope so. It might calm Kev down if they did,' I answered. 'But listen, d'you remember Mark talking about a new guy in his class?'

'The boring one with the computer?'

'Yeah, his name was Gilmartin.' I paused. 'And that's the name of the driver.'

Deirdre shrugged. 'There's probably lots of people called Gilmartin.'

'I suppose so,' I agreed. 'I just wondered.'

'I shouldn't think there's any connection,' said Deirdre, putting the brush back into the bottle of 'Madly Midnight'. 'It's probably your over-active imagination running wild again.'

'You sound just like Miss Kinsella,' I retorted. Though sometimes I wished I didn't have such a vivid imagination. Life would be calmer without it. But duller too.

'Anyway, Mark's supposed to be coming over here soon,' said Deirdre, furiously brushing her already perfect hair in front of the mirror in preparation.

Maybe I'd misjudged her, I thought, and she and Andy really were 'just friends'. 'That's nice,' I said.

'You sound like my mum,' taunted Deirdre. 'She's always telling me what a "nice boy" Mark is. Sorry to disappoint you, but he's only coming to give me a loan of his history notes.'

She's just using him, I thought. But I'd had my say about Mark.

From the jumble of stuff on Deirdre's dressing-table I picked up a bottle of Moisturising Coconut Milk Body Lotion with Added Aloe Vera. '*Leaves the Roughest Skin Silky Smooth*,' I read. 'Is this any good?'

Deirdre shrugged. 'Haven't a clue. Mum gave it to me. It smells good.'

'But does it leave your rough skin silky smooth?'

'Oh yeah,' she said sarcastically. 'Mark's always saying how silky smooth my skin is whenever he kisses my hand.' I thought of Mark polishing his glasses nervously, and I couldn't help laughing.

*   *   *

Downstairs in the hall Fiacla was sitting with her paws folded under her, purring contentedly. I carefully avoided her.

'I'm going to the hospital to see Bernie,' I said to Deirdre. 'Why don't you come?'

She hesitated. 'Is there any point if she's in a coma?'

'Of course there is,' I said heatedly. 'We've got to try and bring her out of it. We're her friends.'

'I know,' said Deirdre. 'But Mark'll be here any minute. And Mum and Dad keep going on about studying and exams.'

'So do mine,' I countered. 'But surely Bernie's more important than all that?'

There was a silence. Then Deirdre said reluctantly, 'I'll go tomorrow, with Ruth.' She sounded as if I had shamed her into it. Even Therese, who was supposed to be Bernie's best friend, hadn't seen Bernie since that first visit. I tried to push down the feeling of resentment towards them all. Why was I the only one, outside of Bernie's family, who felt so involved?

And that brought me back to Kev. 'Better tell Mark to keep his mouth shut if that guy does turn out to be related to the driver,' I said. 'If Kev hears he'll flip.'

Deirdre nodded agreement without arguing, which wasn't like her. Maybe she felt guilty about Bernie, though Deirdre generally wasn't into guilt. She left that to me, I thought, as we parted at her gate. I always felt guilty enough for everyone.

The Awakening

The intensive care unit was becoming as familiar as my own bedroom. The nurse pulled back the curtain around Bernie's cubicle. Mrs Sinnott was by Bernie's bed as usual. When she saw me she tried to smile a greeting. She looked exhausted, but at least she wasn't crying.

'How's she doing?' I whispered.

'The doctor says her breathing has stabilised and they're taking her off the respirator for short periods.'

'Any sign of her coming round?' I asked.

Mrs Sinnott shook her head. 'Her eyes seemed to be flickering this morning,' she said, 'but she didn't open them.'

Bernie lay unmoving, her arm and shoulder strapped up. Her head was still heavily bandaged, but I noticed tiny tendrils of golden hair beginning to grow where it had been shaved. Although her skin was marred by ugly bruises, one side of her face was slightly flushed instead of the dead white it had been before. Trying to be positive, I pointed this out to her mother.

Then I sat beside the bed. 'Hi Bernie,' I said. 'D'you feel

any better today? It's me, Jackie. Everyone's asking for you. Deirdre's coming tomorrow–' I could hear my voice babbling on, till I ran out of things to say. I turned in desperation to Mrs Sinnott.

'Mr Russell, Bernie's teacher was here,' she said quickly. 'He was very nice. They've said special prayers for her in school. He's coming again.' We both looked at Bernie, but there was no response.

There were voices from outside, and the curtains of the cubicle were pulled back. Kev stood there with Sharon and the nurse. He said nothing when he saw me, but I knew he was glad to find me there. Reluctantly, because of the crowd round the bed, I got up to go.

The nurse smiled at me. 'I don't see why you shouldn't all stay,' she said, 'just for a few minutes.' She went back to her desk.

After throwing one frightened glance at Bernie, Sharon climbed on to her mother's lap. 'The doctor said we should try bringing the kids,' Kev muttered to me. 'She thought it might help.'

'I want Bernie to wake up,' Sharon started to cry. Her mother cuddled her and whispered soothingly into her ear. But Sharon wouldn't be pacified. Her cries turned into roars. 'Bernie, I want Bernie!'

The nurse re-appeared. Mrs Sinnott rose, still holding Sharon, and moved away from the bed as the roars grew louder. In the midst of the commotion Kev said urgently, 'Look! Look at Bernie!'

Bernie was moving her head from side to side.

'She heard. I know she heard,' breathed Kev. Sharon

stopped yelling and we were all quiet, gazing at Bernie. She moved her head again. Her face was screwed up, as though she was trying to listen, or speak.

Handing Sharon gently to me, her mother knelt by the bed and held Bernie's hand. 'Bernie, love,' she said. 'Squeeze my hand if you can hear me. Remember, you did it before. Try again.'

Bernie moved her head again, and squeezed her mother's hand. I heard a sharp intake of breath from Kev beside me.

When Sharon saw Bernie move she struggled to go to her. Before anyone could stop her she yelled 'Bernie!' at the top of her voice.

*　　　　*　　　　*

BERNIE

She drifted in and out of a dark void. In the void she was alone. She had vivid dreams of lights changing shape and colour to form different designs, like the kaleidoscope she had once had as a child.

When she came out of the darkness she was aware of pain and anxiety, and a fearful headache. She was haunted by a nagging feeling of having forgotten something important.

There were distant noises, voices talking to her, but although she longed to answer them, she could find no way of communicating. She wasn't in control of her body. She could barely move. Opening her eyes was an impossibly difficult task.

A loud noise. A voice crying, roaring, shouting her name. It was making the headache worse. She moved her head from side to side, trying to block out the noise. But she heard her name being called again and again. She had to speak. She struggled to tell them she could hear them.

The voice calling Bernie rose to a scream. She must see who wanted her so badly. She summoned all her strength. A tremor passed through her body, and her eyes opened.

All she could see was a blur, in which indistinct figures moved. There were so many people, but she couldn't see who they were.

*　　　　*　　　　*

Bernie's eyes shot open. She blinked, as though she couldn't focus properly.

Then she whispered something we couldn't make out. Phlegm rattled in her throat. She gave a choking cough and her thin body shook. When the nurse lifted her into a more comfortable position, Bernie gave a little moan.

We all waited, willing her to speak. Even Sharon, in my arms, was quiet as a mouse.

Her ma, stroking her hand, said softly, 'Talk to us Bernie, love. Try to talk.'

Bernie looked in the direction of her mother's voice. Her eyes were bloodshot. With infinite effort she said hoarsely, 'Why are you ... here?'

For a moment we all stood transfixed. Then Mrs Sinnott said tearfully, 'You've been very sick, love.'

A frown crossed Bernie's face. 'My head ... I can't ...' Her voice faded away.

*   *   *

BERNIE

It had been a huge effort. Had they heard her? Had they understood?

The headache engulfed her, and she drifted thankfully back into the void.

The Argument

I knew by the sudden silence when I entered the kitchen that they had been talking about me. Dad and Nana were sitting at the table over a cup of tea, and Mum had a newspaper spread out on the draining board and was planting bulbs in a bowl.

There was an unmistakable chill in the atmosphere. 'Hi,' I said brightly.

'About time,' snapped Mum. Nana stared straight ahead, sipping her tea daintily.

Even if they're annoyed with me, I thought, surely they'll understand when I explain about Bernie.

'I was at the hospital,' I said. 'And guess what? Bernie actually talked to us!' I waited, but no-one responded. 'She could still have brain damage,' I went on, 'and they can't tell yet if she's paralysed, but the nurse said it was encouraging ...' My voice tailed off.

Dad cleared his throat. 'Of course we're pleased about your friend,' he said.

'Bernie,' I put in sharply. They know her, I thought. Why

can't they say her name?

'However,' he continued heavily, 'you're going to have to give a lot more time to your studies.'

Mum scooped some compost into the bowl and patted it around the bulbs. 'You seem to forget it's an exam year,' she declared. 'At the parent-teacher meeting they said that you should all be working steadily for your mock exams from the first day of term. I've barely seen you lift a finger.'

'It's that crowd from Ballytymon,' chimed in Nana. 'In my opinion Jackie spends far too much time with them.'

'I don't believe this,' I said abruptly. 'Don't any of you realise how sick Bernie's been since the accident? She could have died.' To my dismay, angry tears began to well up, just when I wanted to be cool and calm. Gulping them down I went on, 'It's now she really needs her friends to help carry her through this.'

'We don't mean you're wrong to care about Bernie,' said Dad soothingly. 'There's no need to get upset. But this year is vital for you.'

'It's so important for your future,' added Mum.

'What about Bernie's future?' I retorted. Why couldn't they understand how involved I felt? If they could only see her, I thought desperately, then they'd realise.

Nana brought her cup over to the sink. 'When your mother was at school she used to work night and day,' she intoned. 'I had to beg her to stop and eat.'

Mum laughed uncomfortably. 'Well, it wasn't quite night and day—'

'Oh yes,' Nana continued, 'you were always an excellent student. You took after me.' She looked at me sorrowfully.

Mum took up the attack. 'And this business of missing meals and eating rubbish in McDonald's–'

'That's not fair,' I said hotly. 'It was only that one time after the hospital, when we were all knackered–'

'You see!' Nana pounced. 'You're exhausting yourself with all this hospital business and then you're too tired to study.'

'Anyway,' said Dad, 'we're concerned that you shouldn't get distracted from schoolwork and exams–'

'*Distracted!*' I exploded. 'How would you feel if *I'd* had the accident and was in a coma and Bernie's mum told her she shouldn't care about me because it was too distracting for her?' There was a tense silence.

'We didn't mean–' Mum began.

But I had dashed out of the room and up the stairs before the tears became a flood.

*   *   *

Safe in my room I flung myself on the bed and buried my head in the cool pillow. I lay there as the afternoon light faded. I had to get my head together.

Why was I so angry? I knew Mum and Dad hadn't really meant that Bernie's accident didn't matter. The way they saw it, their duty was to help me do the best I could at school, so that I could have a good career. And to be fair, I hadn't done a thing since term began. The homework and the revision were piling up, and I was falling behind. But how could they expect me just to forget about Bernie, and Kev, and carry on as though the accident hadn't happened?

After a bit there was a tap on the door and Dad came in

and sat on the bed beside me. He patted my shoulder, and pushed a wad of tissues into my hand. As I mopped my face, he said with a rueful grin, 'You have us all in bits. Even Nana's worried about you. "You're too hard on that girl," she told us when you ran out.'

'Well, that's a turn-around,' I snuffled.

'We didn't mean to upset you so much,' he said. 'We know you've been in a state about Bernie.'

I wanted to tell him how I hated feeling so angry and bitter inside. But it was all so complicated. Surely the driver, rather than Mum and Dad, should be the person I was angry with? I could see how you could end up taking out the bitterness on other people when it wasn't even their fault.

And then there was Kev. I knew he felt this bitter rage too. And I was trying to hold him back from doing anything about it. But was it right to bottle it all up? You couldn't do that for ever.

'Dad,' I said, 'Why don't they arrest the driver and charge him with drunken driving, or dangerous driving or something?'

'These things take time,' said Dad. 'The police have to interview witnesses. There has to be enough evidence before they can go ahead.'

'But nothing seems to be happening to him at all. They just breathalysed him and let him go,' I protested. 'And when you think what he did–'

We were interrupted by a scuffling outside my door. Dad rose and opened it. I couldn't believe my eyes. Philip was tiptoeing towards his own room. Grasping his hand firmly was a tall lanky girl peering short-sightedly through very thick glasses. Her hair was in long curls tied up with two pink bows. The two of them were clutching thick sheaves of paper.

'Well, Philip,' said Dad, 'Aren't you going to introduce us to your friend?'

Philip looked bashful, something new for him. The girl said, in loud piercing tones, 'I'm Mary Rose Brennan, and I'm in the play with Phil.'

'Phil?' repeated Dad, puzzled.

I nudged him. 'She means Philip. She must be Robin.' Dad looked bewildered.

'Yes, that's right,' she explained. 'Robin Hood.' She beamed. 'And Phil's Maid Marian.'

'And what are you doing here exactly?' enquired Dad.

'We're going to rehearse,' she shrilled. 'We need somewhere private.' And she marched into Philip's bedroom, yanking him after her.

Dad stared after them. 'I'm just not able for this,' he said. 'I'd better get Mum.'

He disappeared downstairs, and I sat down at my desk. I realised I felt a bit better. The tight angry feeling had eased for the moment. Maybe the way to deal with it was to talk about it, get it off your chest, let it out. If only Kev could do that more, I thought, he might feel better too. Most of the time he kept things locked up inside him.

When I'd had big problems, I'd confided in Kev, and he'd listened. But I also had Deirdre and the others, and Bernie, and sometimes Mum and Dad.

But Kev only had Bernie and me to turn to. Now there

was just me. And it was so rare for him to talk about how he felt. But when he did, like that night in the garden, I felt needed and important to him. It made up for all the difficult times. And maybe it helped diffuse the anger that was simmering dangerously in him, just below the surface.

*   *   *

Dwelling on Kev made my mind spin back to that amazing moment in the hospital only a few hours before.

When Bernie had spoken, we'd all stood there stunned.

'That's the best response we've had so far,' said the nurse, pleased. 'I'll notify Dr Murray.' She looked at Sharon, who was rubbing her tear-stained face with grubby fingers. 'Well, Sharon, it was you who brought your sister round. Well done.'

Sharon put her thumb in her mouth and hung on to Kev. 'Fair play to you,' he said to her, smiling.

Bernie had closed her eyes and seemed to be sleeping peacefully. We all filed out except Mrs Sinnott. 'I'll stay a little longer,' she said.

Outside, the nurse told us that when Bernie woke again they would be testing for brain damage. 'The doctor will check if she can move her limbs, and we'll try to find out how much she remembers,' she told us, as she went off to get Mrs Sinnott a cup of tea.

'Well, it's a start,' said Kev. He put one arm round me and the other round Sharon and we headed off down the corridor. I was filled with joy.

But as usual there was no time to talk. He was rushing to catch the Ballytymon bus to bring Sharon home, and I was already late too. We parted with a hasty kiss on the cheek.

On the way home I had reflected hopefully that Bernie's improvement might help to stop Kev brooding about the driver, Arthur Gilmartin.

*   *   *

Muffled thumps from Philip's room brought me back to the present. There was obviously some serious rehearsing going on.

I got out *The Playboy of the Western World* again, and turned to Act One, Scene One. This time I was determined I wasn't going to let it defeat me. I forced my mind away from Kev and Bernie, and on to Pegeen Mike and the fella who killed his Da.

The Talk

Following on Saturday's row, everyone at home was careful to be extra nice to everyone else. Gran and Nana came for Sunday lunch as usual, and Nana made a point of asking about 'your friend Bernadette'. It took me a second to work out who she meant.

Dad asked Philip how the rehearsals were going.

'Mary Rose said Miss Cassidy told her I was a natural actor,' he bragged. 'And Mary Rose's mum's going to do my make-up for me.'

Nana opened her mouth, presumably to make a sharp remark about Philip wearing make-up. But catching Dad's eye, she changed it into a yawn.

'How nice,' said Gran. 'I'm sure you'll look sweet.' Philip looked far from happy at the idea of 'looking sweet'. In the interests of this new era of politeness I refrained from asking Philip if he and Mary Rose had something going, or if he still thought she was mouldy-looking.

*   *   *

As a result of all this, there was no problem popping off for an hour to meet the gang, especially as I'd spent most of the day dutifully studying.

Outside Pizza Paradise, waiting for Deirdre, a recollection flashed into my mind of the day of Bernie's accident. Looking around it was hard to believe what had happened so near here just over a week before, and how much everything had changed since then.

As we sat round the table drinking Diet Cokes I asked Deirdre and Ruth if Bernie had been awake when they were at the hospital. They exchanged glances.

'She was sitting up and her eyes were open,' said Ruth. She hesitated.

Deirdre went on, 'But she didn't seem too sure who we were.' I stared at her in shock.

Deirdre added quickly, 'I don't think she could see us properly. And she was in pain from the fracture. The nurse said she was heavily sedated, and that could make her confused.'

'Did she speak to you?'

'She said something about someone waiting for her,' said Ruth, 'but she couldn't remember who it was. She kept forgetting words all the time.' I had a sinking feeling.

'The doctor said it was amnesia, and it's very common after what she called a trauma,' said Deirdre. 'Remember, I told you about it before.' She had, but I hadn't taken much notice. Then, the important thing was for Bernie to come round. I'd somehow thought that once she woke up and spoke, everything would be all right again.

But now I wondered if Bernie would ever be the same

again. I pictured her, calm and kind, marching along with her fair hair swinging, reassuring me about Kev, taking care of her sisters, dashing to the supermarket after school when her ma was sick so that there'd be something in for the tea.

'Was her ma there, or Kev?' I asked.

'No. The nurse said their ma wasn't feeling well.'

This was even worse news. Things must be very difficult at home if their mother was sick, on top of everything else. If only I could talk to Kev, maybe I could help, I thought. I'd heard nothing from him since the hospital the day before. Was he still raging about the driver? How could I get in touch with him? If I took a chance on going to his house in Ballytymon, he might not even be there. Maybe I could write to him. But that would take time. I heaved a sigh. Why was everything was so complicated?

'Jackie, you look as if you're carrying the troubles of the world on your shoulders,' said Deirdre as I stared into space.

I tried to lighten up. 'Um, did Mark come round yesterday with the history notes?'

'Oh yeah.' She sounded unenthusiastic. 'They weren't much use. There were pages of that shiny computer paper with lots of smudgy little graphics. I couldn't be bothered reading them.'

'What's Mark up to these days?' asked Ruth.

Deirdre shrugged. 'He's pretty useless too,' she said. She went to put some money in the video jukebox.

Ruth caught my eye. It looked like Mark was for the chop again. The history notes hadn't helped.

'I hope this doesn't mean you're going back with Andy,' groaned Ruth, as 'Look at Me' flashed up on the video. 'He's such a big-head.'

'What about that girl Monika, in Germany?' I asked. 'Are you sure they've broken up?'

'Monika?' said Deirdre. 'That's been over for ages.'

'I suppose it was the present you got from Andy that did it,' I said nastily to Deirdre.

'What present?' asked Ruth.

Deirdre turned on me. 'Jackie, you're always in such a foul mood these days,' she snapped. 'You've been like that since Bernie's accident. You act as if it was our fault.' And she jumped up and marched out of the café.

*   *   *

I hate my life, I thought that evening as I wearily packed up my school books for Monday morning. Nothing had gone right since Bernie's accident. Problems were piling up like stormclouds. And now Deirdre was pissed off with me as well.

I sat on my bed, trying to plan what to do about everything. Then I thought about Therese. She lived near the Sinnotts. Tomorrow in school I would talk to her and find out what was happening there, and if there was anything I could do. Then I'd have to try and make it up with Deirdre.

That's if nothing else crops up between now and then, I reflected, as I crawled into bed.

The Shock

'Come on, girls, let's blow those cobwebs away!' called Miss Doherty, the PE teacher, who was cheerful and tireless and appeared to be under the delusion that we were all aiming at Olympic gold medals, or at least the all-Ireland athletics.

We crouched shivering beside the running track as the sharp east wind whipped the first fallen leaves around the field. 'I've got goose pimples,' grumbled Ruth.

'Exercise and fresh air are good for tension and stress,' Deirdre said, throwing me a look. This was Deirdre's way of showing she'd accepted my effort to make up after our earlier row.

'Yeah,' I agreed dutifully, my teeth chattering.

'Now, Jackie,' called Miss Doherty, 'Show us how fit you are after the holidays. I'm sure you did lots of jogging.'

I felt my knees cracking as I straightened up and tried to assume a Sonia O'Sullivan position. I could hear giggles from Therese and Ruth as I started off, breathing heavily and wincing at the sharp pains in my ankles. I must be the least fit person in the class, I thought despondently. After the first few minutes, I had gradually slowed almost to a walking pace. Through the buzzing in my ears I could hear encouraging cries from Miss Doherty. Finally staggering to a halt, I threw myself on the grass, gasping for breath.

'Um, well tried,' said Miss Doherty, without much conviction.

Therese came and sat beside me. 'You're going to have to do a lot more practice if you want to get that medal,' she said sarcastically. We watched Deirdre running effortlessly round the track, her slim legs in white shorts moving rhythmically up and down like pistons. I was stabbed by a recollection of Bernie lying immobile in her hospital bed.

'Did you hear about the way Bernie was when the others went to see her?' I asked Therese.

She nodded. 'The doctor said the amnesia would probably get better,' she said.

'Hope she's right,' I said, massaging my legs. 'What's happening at the Sinnotts'?'

'Their ma's nerves are bad,' said Therese. 'They're all shattered. Kev barely says a word to anyone. All the neighbours are calling in, and their aunt's minding the kids, but it's a real mess.'

'I was thinking of calling round there,' I said hesitantly, 'to see if there was anything I could do.'

'Come home with me on Wednesday when we finish early,' said Therese. 'We could go there together.' I felt better immediately at the prospect of at least trying to help. And it would be easier with Therese along. Some of her assertiveness might rub off on me.

'Thanks a million, Therese.' But as I said it, I realised that if I went to the hospital the next day, as I'd planned, and to Ballytymon with Therese on the day after that, there would certainly be more trouble at home. The period of sweetness and light we'd had after the big argument was already wearing thin, and I doubted if it was going to last much longer.

Ruth threw herself down beside us, her face scarlet. 'I don't know how Deirdre does it,' she protested. 'How can she stay so fit when she eats all the wrong things?'

Deirdre strolled up munching a Yorkie. 'You see!' hissed Ruth.

Therese jumped to her feet. 'Let's get some pizza in the shopping centre on the way home,' she said. 'We need to keep our strength up after all that exercise.'

'Good idea,' we chorused.

'But the cholesterol–' began Ruth. She stopped when she saw our expressions.

Leaning on each other, we tottered in to get our bags.

*   *   *

BERNIE

There used to be someone sitting beside the bed most of the time. Sometimes she talked to Bernie in a low voice. Often she wept quietly. Bernie sensed it was her mother, but when she opened her eyes she could only see a blurred figure. She tried to tell her she was going to be all right. Sometimes Bernie found she could speak, but other times the words flew away, or they came out in the wrong order.

But now her mother had disappeared. And the fair-haired boy she thought she knew, who used to come for a little while around the time the food trolleys rattled outside in the corridor. He never said much, but she knew he was unhappy. She waited for him every day. But he didn't come either.

'Well, Bernie, how are you today, dear?' She could see a figure in white. 'What's my name, Bernie? Can you remember?' The familiar voice of the kind nurse. She told Bernie her name every day. Bernie hated to disappoint the nurse. She tried to dredge it out of her memory. But it was no good. It was gone. And her shoulder was hurting. All her body hurt, it was one big ache. Her head was worst of all.

The nurse sponged her gently. Then she helped Bernie to sip a sweet milky drink.

Someone came in, a man. She thought he'd been before.

'Hallo, Bernie. It's Mr Russell, from school. How are you doing?' The voice was nice, kind, cheerful.

Trying to focus on the owner, she struggled to summon words. 'Red,' she said. 'Your–' The word escaped her. She made another attempt. 'What ... you're wearing,' she managed. 'Red.'

He laughed, and so did the nurse. She knew they were pleased.

'Right, Bernie,' he said. 'My wife despairs of this red sweatshirt. The first time it was washed it turned everything pink. The whole family has pink underwear now.'

Bernie tried to laugh, but it hurt too much. A groan came out instead. They stopped laughing. 'She's due an injection,' said the nurse. 'The collar-bone is very painful.'

'And the bruising, I suppose,' said the teacher, with a sigh. He raised his voice. 'I'll pop in again soon, pet. Everyone at school is asking for you.'

Bernie wanted to ask about her mother, and the boy. And a memory came and went of children, little girls, who she used to mind.

She had forgotten the teacher's name. But she must have forced something out, because the nurse said soothingly. 'Your ma's not well. Nothing serious, just a touch of flu. She'll be in to see you again soon.'

Bernie felt the prick of a needle in her arm, and the pain slowly began to float away.

She slept.

*   *   *

Through my recurring dream about speeding cars and wailing sirens, I could hear a distant bell ringing. As I struggled up through layers of sleep, the sound grew louder. At first I thought it was my alarm clock, and I reached out to turn it off. Then I realised it was the phone downstairs.

Yawning, I looked at my watch. It was 3 am. Who could be phoning at this hour? I went out and stood on the landing. All the bedroom doors were shut, and no-one else appeared to have heard. Pattering downstairs in bare feet, a shiver of anxiety passed through me. Was it Nana, or Gran?

Nervously, I picked up the phone. 'Hallo?'

There were confused sounds from the other end, but no-one spoke. Maybe it was one of the crank calls I'd heard about. I was about to hang up when a voice said abruptly, 'Jackie?'

'Kev?' I said doubtfully. 'Is that you?' I could hear voices in the background, and a phone ringing.

'Jackie,' he said again. Something in his tone frightened me.

'Kev, where are you? What's wrong?'

Images coursed wildly through my mind. Someone taken ill? Another accident? Then the most horrific thought of all. 'Is it Bernie?'

'No, she's okay.' He was silent. Then he said hoarsely, 'I'm in the station.'

'The station?' Was he going away?

'Rathnure Garda Station,' he went on. 'I've been arrested.'

'Oh, no!' I could feel my heart banging. The vague threat I'd feared for so long had taken shape. What had he done?

'Kev,' I stammered. 'Are you all right?'

'I'm okay,' he said. He sounded strange, different.

'Are you sure?' I said. 'Shall I come down there?' I made myself ask him, 'Why did they arrest you?'

'It was him, Gilmartin, the driver,' he said in a rush. 'Jackie, I couldn't stand it any longer. I had to do something.'

I sank down on to the stairs. 'Kev, tell me,' I said quietly. '*What* did you do?'

The Attack

There was no way I was going to get back to sleep after that phone-call from the garda station. I drew back the curtains and looked out at the garden, recalling the night Kev had come. Now the moon was hidden behind clouds and the branches of the apple tree swayed in the gusts of wind.

Was there something I could have said or done that night that might have prevented this latest disaster? On the phone Kev had said very little, just that he'd been at the Gilmartins' house and had been caught. It wasn't clear what he'd actually done, or how serious it was.

He'd had to hang up, and I'd waited by the phone till he rang again about half an hour later. This time he'd said he was going to be released, and would have to appear in Rathnure Court at half past ten the next morning.

'Where are you going now?' I asked fearfully.

'Don't worry,' he said, to my relief. 'I've been in enough trouble for one night. I'm off home.'

'Are you going to tell your ma?' Poor woman, I thought,

Kev in trouble was going to be more than she could take.

'No way,' he answered. 'She's in Loman's for treatment so she won't hear anything about it.'

'Is there anything I can do?' I asked. It sounded so stilted, but my brain seemed to have seized up.

'No.' His voice shook. 'I shouldn't have called really, it's just that when they said I could make a call, you were–' He stopped. In spite of everything my heart lifted.

'Kev, it's okay,' I said. 'I'm glad you phoned. What about lawyers and that stuff? D'you need money?' My thoughts raced ahead. Maybe I should tell Mum and Dad what had happened, and see if they could help. But they'd go berserk at my being mixed up in something like this.

'They said I could ask the judge for legal aid. That means I might be able to have a lawyer for free.' Kev paused. 'Don't tell your mum and dad. They won't understand.'

How could he read my thoughts over the phone? I thought back to the row with my parents. Maybe Kev was right. If they considered my involvement in Bernie's accident distracting, what were they going to say about this? After all, whatever Kev had done, it was serious enough for him to have to appear in court.

'Gotta go,' he mumbled. 'I'll try and let you know what happens.' And the phone went dead.

I turned from the window. I was freezing and my foot had gone to sleep.

Back in bed my mind jumped from Kev to Bernie. I hadn't seen her since Saturday. She must be feeling terrible, with the pain and the amnesia. And now her mum was sick and Kev was in serious trouble. I had to get to see her the next day.

But Kev needed me too. He had no-one else, and he'd turned to me. I was determined to be there when he appeared in court. I couldn't leave him to face that alone.

And where did all this leave school, study and exams? To go to court I'd have to do something I'd never done before, I'd have to mitch from school.

And I might be found out.

The Court

'There's a letter for you, Jackie,' announced Dad, putting down *The Irish Times* as I came in for breakfast. 'It's from the gardaí.'

'The gardaí?' Could they be looking for me because of Kev and last night's events? My mind was so preoccupied with devising a way to get to the court that morning for Kev's appearance, that it took a moment before I copped on.

'It must be about Bernie,' I said.

'Unless you've been involved in some crime that we don't know about,' said Dad. I nearly choked on my orange juice. 'Joke,' he said grinning. I smiled weakly and looked down at the letter.

'It's from a sergeant at Rathnure Garda Station,' I told him. 'They want me to come down to make a statement about the accident.'

'But I thought you didn't actually see what happened,' said Mum, putting bread in the toaster. 'I can't see what help you'd be.'

'And it'll take up more time,' agreed Dad. 'But I suppose it has to be done.'

Philip, who had been muttering to himself in between spooning up his Frosties, burst out, 'I'm fed up with everyone going on about Jackie around here.'

So am I, I thought.

'No-one bothers about me, even though I'm the star in the school play,' he whinged, 'and I've only got another two days before the dress rehearsal.'

'Of course we're interested, Philip,' said Mum. 'Aren't we all busy with your costume, even Gran?'

'You still haven't got me the hipsters,' he said accusingly. Dad snorted.

'I'm going into town tomorrow,' said Mum. 'I'll have a look in the ILAC Centre.'

'Mary Rose says hipsters are cool,' declared Philip.

'*Were* cool,' I corrected.

'Surely you should have green tights?' asked Dad seriously.

'No, Mary Rose and the Merry Men are wearing those,' said Philip. 'And Mary Rose's getting her sister's high-heeled boots and her dad's gardening gloves.'

As they all chatted brightly about Philip's play, I was thinking furiously. I planned to go to school as usual, and then try and slip away after commerce class. That should give me half an hour to get to the court-house. I wasn't sure of the address, but it was too risky to ask anyone, even Deirdre.

I looked at my watch and mumbled something about getting to school early. As I put on my coat in the hall, my stomach was so churned up with the mixture of fear and guilt that I thought I was going to be sick.

From the kitchen I could hear Philip's shrill tones as he read his lines to Mum and Dad. Quietly I closed the front door behind me.

*　　　*　　　*

My breath came in painful gasps as I panted up the road to the court-house. It was nearly eleven. At school I'd discovered there was a staff meeting starting at break, so at least I wasn't missing class. But it had been tricky getting away, and someone might notice my non-appearance at the study period.

I'd had a problem finding the place. Looking ahead I couldn't see any big building that resembled my idea of a court-house. Then I noticed people milling about in a yard beside what looked like a small church set back from the road. I entered the open gate to ask directions.

The first person I saw was Kev. He was standing in a little group, which included his uncle, another man I didn't know and, to my amazement, Andy. Kev's jaw dropped when he spotted me. 'What're you doing here?'

'I'm on the hop,' I answered breathlessly. 'I thought you'd be on your own.'

'Yeah well, my uncle heard me coming in last night, so I had to tell him,' he said. 'And we met Andy on the bus on the way here. He said he'd come with me.'

'So I needn't have come.' A wave of disappointment washed over me.

'No,' said Kev quickly. 'I'm really glad you came.' He

touched my shoulder gently.

Andy stood with his hands in the pockets of his black Levi's. I had to admit he looked cool, his cropped hair emphasising his good looks. 'You missed the show,' he said.

'D'you mean it's all over? Already?'

'It's adjourned,' said Kev's uncle. 'It'll be on this day week.'

'But what happened?'

'The garda said he'd arrested Kev last night and charged him with malicious damage. He said Kev had admitted it. Kev pleaded guilty. Then they arranged legal aid.'

I went cold. 'Malicious damage to what?'

Kev said quietly, 'Gilmartin's house. I threw a brick through his window.'

I was speechless. Kev, who always spoke so softly, who was so gentle when he touched me or kissed me! I just couldn't imagine him doing something so violent.

But then I remembered the other Kev, raging about his dad and what he'd done to their mother, telling me fiercely how angry he was with the driver of the car that had nearly destroyed his sister, and the way the driver seemed to be untouched by the whole incident.

'Was anyone hurt?' I asked fearfully.

Kev said nothing. He was gripping the railing beside him tightly. His uncle looked at him and said, 'No, thanks be to God. A kitchen window was broken. The young lad heard it and came out and found Kev in the garden.'

'The young lad?' I asked.

'Gilmartin's son,' said Kev. He spoke in a sudden rush.

'He's got red hair, like the father. He grabbed me. I was going to punch him. I think I shouted something about the accident, and Bernie. He let go then. He didn't seem to know what I was talking about.' He heaved a quivering sigh, as though it was a relief to get it all out. He added quietly, 'Then I just waited there till the gardaí came.'

'You waited there?' said the other man, who I realised must be the lawyer. 'Why didn't you run away?'

Kev looked at him directly. 'Why should I?' he said. 'I'm not denying what I did. I had to do something, and it could've been a lot worse.' He swallowed hard. 'It's nothing compared to what he did to Bernie.'

For a moment, no-one spoke. The image I could never forget, of Bernie lying on the road with blood seeping through her shining hair, flashed back into my mind.

The lawyer said, 'Whatever the provocation, we can't take the law into our own hands.'

'Even if the driver gets away with it?' said Kev, almost inaudibly.

'He won't. He'll be punished,' said the lawyer. 'You just have to be patient.'

'But he was over the limit,' insisted Kev. 'Bernie nearly died. And he's just let go home.' Standing close to him I could feel his anger. His whole body was trembling.

'He was allowed out on bail. That doesn't mean he's going to get off scot-free,' said the lawyer patiently. 'The case against him can't go ahead till all the evidence has been gathered from the witnesses. The gardaí have to make sure the case is strong enough to get him convicted.'

Kev didn't reply. I had a powerful urge to touch him,

hold him, even in front of everyone.

I made myself put my fear into words. 'What's going to happen to Kev?' I asked the lawyer.

'He has to come back next week,' answered the lawyer. 'In the meantime the judge'll get a probationer's report on Kev.' Turning to Kev and his uncle he went on, 'We'd better fix up an appointment for you to come to my office.'

It wasn't a very satisfactory reply. I didn't like to ask what a probationer's report was. But the lawyer's tone was quiet and reassuring. He even gave a dry little smile.

*　　　　*　　　　*

Leaving the two men at the court, Andy, Kev and I headed off down the road in a heavy silence. I'd assumed that, for better or worse, the whole situation was going to be settled when Kev appeared in court. But his ordeal still lay ahead.

I cast a glance at him, and our eyes met. I remembered The Look, the first time we'd ever seen each other.

He cleared his throat. 'I suppose you think I shouldn't–' he began. But before he could finish Andy chimed in, 'There's someone called Gilmartin in that stupid sap Mark's class.'

'Mark's not a sap,' I snapped. 'And he's far from stupid.'

'Deirdre doesn't think Mark's so great,' said Andy mockingly. 'She's coming to the pictures with me on Saturday.'

'Everything was fine with Deirdre and Mark till you showed up,' I said sharply to Andy.

'Don't worry about Mark,' sneered Andy. 'He's always got his computer for company.'

Before I could answer Kev stopped. 'Is that true? Is there

someone called Gilmartin in Mark's class?' His tone held a threat.

'Mark says there's a guy with that name,' I said quickly. 'But I don't think he's any relation.'

'He'd better not be,' Kev flashed back.

Let's hope he isn't, I thought. We've all got enough problems.

When we reached the bus stop I glared at Andy, willing him to buzz off and leave us alone. I needed to talk to Kev, and there wasn't much time. But Andy didn't move.

Trying to ignore him, I turned to Kev. 'I wish I didn't have to rush back to school.'

'Yeah,' he said, 'I hope you don't get into trouble.'

I gazed desperately at him. I wanted so much to comfort him and tell him not to worry, that the lawyer would help him, that I would always stand by him, but that he mustn't do anything else that could make things worse. But I couldn't say those things with Andy there, with his mocking smile.

We stood in a tense silence. After a minute Kev said urgently to me, 'Can you get in to see Bernie tonight? I have to stay late to make up the class I missed this morning.'

'Don't worry, I'm going to the hospital straight after school—'

Andy interrupted. 'Do they know at the course about what you did, Kev?'

'Not so far,' said Kev shortly. 'I suppose they'll find out.' As the bus trundled up Kev mumbled, 'Thanks for coming, Jackie.' He paused. 'About Bernie, too.' And in spite of Andy's leering presence, he bent down and kissed me on the lips. All my worries about what Kev had done, my mitching from school, exasperation with Andy, drifted away as a kind of melting softness flowed through me.

But as soon as I sat down on the bus, other, more unpleasant problems zoomed in on me. First I had to get back into school without being noticed. At least I'd be back before lunch, and I'd only missed one study period, I tried to reassure myself. But I still felt guilty. And, even if no-one else noticed, Deirdre and the others would certainly expect an explanation.

Then, if I went to see Bernie after school, I was going to be late home again. That was sure to mean another row. And I had to figure out how to get back to the court for Kev's case next week.

But above everything else loomed the vital question. What was going to happen to Kev?

The Stranger

BERNIE

She was lying in her bed being wheeled along corridors, and into a lift, which rose upwards with a low hum. Staring up at the ceiling she felt cocooned, like a baby in a pram. The cheery porter in a blue coat kept repeating to her, 'Don't you worry about a thing. You're going to be just fine.' Everyone said that to her constantly.

But Bernie did worry. Why was there so much she couldn't remember? People's names, who they were exactly, how she came to be in this place.

People fed her mushy food, sponged her body, changed dressings, and gently massaged and moved her limbs. They talked about an accident and fractures and bruising, but no-one explained what had happened or if they had, she'd forgotten. She had a hazy memory of being in a shop with a little child, and then hurrying to meet someone. There had been a loud insistent noise. After that it was as though a curtain had dropped.

'Welcome to ward B7, Bernie,' said a brisk voice. 'I'm

sure you're glad to be out of the intensive care.' Bernie could see that under her starched white cap the nurse had long silky fair hair just like her own, tied back in a ponytail.

The nurse adjusted the bed and propped her up. Looking round she saw three other beds. From the bed opposite a young woman smiled a welcome. Sunshine poured into the room and through the window Bernie could see a tree, sharp and clear, some of its leaves just turning an orangey-red.

Things aren't so blurred any more, she thought, I can see better. She looked at the nurse and pointed to the window. But the words wouldn't come.

'Yes, Bernie,' said the nurse, smiling, 'it's a lovely sunny day.'

Bernie tried to smile back. Surely if she concentrated she would be able to reply. But her head was starting to throb, and her shoulder hurt.

She drifted off into an uneasy doze.

*   *   *

'You have a visitor,' the nurse announced, rousing Bernie from a dream in which she was running along a beach, with little waves breaking over her bare feet. She whimpered, reluctant to leave the dream and face reality.

Maybe it's my mother, she thought, the one person she remembered. Pain darted through her as she struggled to sit up. She turned to the doorway expectantly.

A fella of about her own age tip-toed into the ward. He was holding a bunch of yellow flowers. A shadow of disappointment crossed Bernie's face. It wasn't her mother, or those girls who came sometimes, or even the other boy, vaguely familiar to her, who used to stand by her bed looking at her anxiously.

But maybe she really knew this person, and had forgotten him like so many other people and things. She watched him approach her bedside. She noticed he had red hair.

'Er, Bernie Sinnott?' he asked hesitantly. 'My name's Greg Gilmartin.'

The Flowers

'Lots of visitors today, Bernie,' said the nurse brightly, as she brought me over to Bernie's bed. I sank down on to the chair beside it, hot and exhausted.

'Just dashing off to see Bernie,' I'd called to the gang as I hurried out of school, knowing they were desperate to hear why I'd disappeared that morning and slipped back in at lunch-time. But I wasn't ready to tell them yet. Anyway, there was no time.

Redirected from the intensive care unit, I'd wandered along corridors and zoomed up and down in lifts, glimpsing patients in dressing-gowns, chattering nurses, people in white coats talking into bleepers just like in 'ER'. Eventually I'd found Ward B7.

Bernie was sitting up in bed with her arm in a sling, and I noticed that for the first time she was wearing a nightdress instead of the hospital tunic. A large dressing had replaced the bandage round her head.

There was a vase of yellow flowers on the locker beside her. Her blue eyes, still bloodshot, were enormous in her thin face. But they had lost that vague unfocused look. 'Who's ... he?' she began agitatedly when she saw me. 'What does he ...?' Her speech was jerky, with pauses between the words.

'Who, Bernie?' I asked, puzzled. 'D'you mean Kev? He wasn't here, was he?'

'The fella. The other ... one, not–' Her eyes willed me to understand.

The nurse in the intensive care had warned me that Bernie had suffered some brain damage, and her memory and her grasp of words might not come back for a while. The nurse hadn't said how long, and I hadn't been able to bring myself to ask.

'Was he someone in a dream, this fella?' I asked her.

She shook her head impatiently. 'He talked ... He said–' She stopped, tears of frustration rolling down her cheeks.

I felt tears coming to my eyes too. I longed to tell her about Kev and the awful trouble he was in. But I knew it was impossible. Before all this, Bernie used to comfort and calm me down when things went wrong. Now, when she needed me, I couldn't even understand her, let alone calm her.

Remembering Therese's instructions about dealing with stress, I drew a deep breath. I took Bernie's hand, which was discoloured with bruises from the injections. I said quietly, 'Bernie, it's okay.'

I was amazed my voice could sound so soothing when my mind was in such a turmoil. 'Just rest for a minute,' I went on, 'and then tell me slowly about the fella.'

I could see she'd understood. Her body relaxed, and she

whispered, ' ... Sorry.' Only Bernie, I reflected, would reach through all that pain and confusion to apologise.

'It's not your fault, Bernie,' I said. 'None of this is your fault.'

I added silently, It's Arthur Gilmartin's fault.

*   *   *

After a moment, Bernie gripped my hand with her good one. Then she said slowly, 'A strange fella ... with red ...'

'A red T-shirt?' I suggested. She shook her head, and for a second I recalled how her long fair hair used to swing from side to side whenever she did that.

'Nice,' she brought out. 'He was ... nice.' And she pointed to the flowers.

'Nice,' I agreed. Kev must've got in after all, or maybe a friend or neighbour, and they'd brought her flowers.

I rose. 'I've got to go home and study, Bernie,' I said. 'Otherwise I'll be in trouble.' The understatement of the year, I thought to myself.

She reached out and touched my hand. Closing her eyes tight in concentration she whispered, 'Thanks ... you came.'

'Kev'll probably be in tomorrow,' I said. She looked at me questioningly. 'Kev,' I repeated. 'Your brother. The fella.' She nodded uncertainly.

I was fairly sure there was no way she would get to hear the news about Kev. I knew he hadn't told her, but even if she'd heard, she probably wouldn't be able to understand. If only it could all get sorted out somehow, so that neither Bernie nor their ma need ever hear about it. But I knew there wasn't a hope.

As I turned to leave, the nurse from the intensive care appeared. She said cheerfully to Bernie. 'Hi, Bernie, it's me, from the intensive care where you were before,' she said. 'Can you remember my name? I told you this morning.'

Bernie frowned, and shut her eyes. Then she shook her head sadly. 'No ... sorry.'

'Never mind,' said the nurse. 'One of these days you will.'

At the entrance to the ward I looked back. Bernie was gazing after me. She gave a little, wistful smile.

And for a second, I recognised a flash of the old Bernie.

The Call

I trudged towards home, my limbs heavy with ex-haus- tion, my mind whirling with the events of the day. First, getting out of school, then the court, then the argument with Andy, and finally the disturbing visit to Bernie.

But as I got closer to home, a new debate surfaced in my mind. Should I tell Mum and Dad about Kev? Judging by the last row, I was sure they would react immediately and negatively before I had a chance to explain the whole story. And if I did explain, they might not understand why Kev had done what he did. They might even try and stop me seeing Kev or Bernie, just when they both needed me most.

But they'd have to know sooner or later. A voice in my mind whispered, better later than sooner.

* * *

'Hi, Jackie,' squeaked a high-pitched voice as I reached our house.

Sitting on the front wall, where I had sat so many times

with Kev and the others, were Philip, his friend Conor, and Philip's 'mouldy-looking' co-star, Mary Rose.

I was too tired and fed up to respond to her greeting, but that didn't faze her.

'Phil's invited me to tea,' she shrilled. 'My mummy thinks he's a really lovely boy.'

'Philip?' I said in disbelief. 'Lovely? Are you serious?' I could think of lots of words to describe Philip, but 'lovely' wasn't one of them.

Mary Rose jumped down from the wall with a broad grin which showed her gums and all her teeth, including a gold one at the back. She was in her Robin Hood emerald green tights with two matching green bows in her hair.

'Hey Jackie,' said Philip excitedly, 'you'll never guess what's happened about the play!'

'What?' I said ungraciously. Conor, Philip's friend, unaffected by the excitement, sat on the wall chewing rhythmically.

'From now on,' Mary Rose paused dramatically, 'we've got to improvise.'

'Improvise?'

'It means we've to make it up as we go along,' explained Philip. 'Teacher says our lines sounded all wrong and everyone would laugh when they're not s'posed to.' Recalling the rehearsal I'd overheard, I silently agreed with teacher.

'So we've got to make it sound more – what did she say, Phil?'

'Natural,' said Philip, smiling fondly at Mary Rose. She grabbed his hand and yanked him off the wall.

'Teacher told the class the success of the whole play

depends on Maid Marian and Robin,' she went on. 'Didn't she, Conor?' Conor stared into space impassively, still chewing.

'Are Mum and Dad in?' I asked Philip.

'No, they're at the parent-teacher meeting,' answered Philip. That was a relief. I didn't have the energy to talk to them, let alone have a row about being late. I plodded wearily into the house, leaving Philip staring up adoringly at Mary Rose, while Conor sat on, alone with his chewing gum.

*   *   *

'Jackie, it's Mark.' I had run downstairs when I heard the phone, hoping it was Kev.

I hadn't got very far with my maths, but at least when my parents had arrived home from the parent-teacher meeting they had found me studying.

'Mark?' A call from him was unusual. 'Hi, how're you?'

'Okay.' He sounded nervous. 'It's about that guy in my class, Greg Gilmartin.'

Alarm bells sounded in my mind. 'What about him?'

'He'd been out of school for a while, but he was back in today.' Mark cleared his throat.

'Yeah?' I prompted.

'The man who knocked Bernie down,' he said in a rush. 'It was Greg's dad.'

The Connection

Back upstairs in my room Mark's news about his friend Greg echoed in my mind.

Maybe it was unfair, but I could only feel hostility towards anyone with such a close connection to the driver who had injured Bernie. At the same time I couldn't help feeling intense interest in this Greg.

'What did he say about the accident?' I had asked Mark.

'He said his dad just told them at home that there'd been a minor accident and someone was slightly hurt,' answered Mark. 'Greg nearly freaked when I told him the full story.'

'Didn't he know about his dad being breathalysed, and that he was over the limit?'

'Well, he said his dad often comes home drunk,' said Mark. He paused. 'But he also told me something else–' There was a meaningful silence. I waited tensely for Mark's next question.

'Jackie,' he continued hesitantly, 'Greg told me someone smashed their window the other night. Greg caught him and the gardaí came and arrested him. Greg didn't know who he was but it had something to do with the accident.'

'Yeah,' I said, after a moment. There was no point in trying to hide it now. Once Mark knew the whole crowd was going to hear.

'You know about it?' said Mark. 'Then it was Kev?'

I tried to find the words to explain. 'Kev was so furious. He needed to hit out at someone.' My voice shook. 'And now he's in serious trouble.'

There was a silence. 'I figured it must have been him,' said Mark slowly. 'I hope they're not too heavy on him. I know he shouldn't have done it, but he must be in bits about Bernie.'

'Yeah, *we* understand that,' I said. 'But what about the judge? He'll just see Kev as someone who deliberately smashed a window.'

'Surely Kev'll get a chance to explain? About Bernie and everything?'

'Even if he does it mightn't help,' I said, recalling the lawyer's warning about not taking the law into your own hands. 'Although apparently the judge gets some kind of report about Kev's family situation before the case comes up.'

'Maybe that'll help,' said Mark.

'I suppose this Greg fella's raging with Kev?' I asked.

'You'd think so,' said Mark. 'But now he knows what really happened it's his dad he's raging with. He said his mum did her best to persuade his dad to get help for his drink problem, but he would never accept that he had one, let alone do anything about it.'

'Was there trouble before with him drinking?'

'It's been going on for years. And he's sometimes violent,' said Mark. 'But this is the first time he's been done for drink driving.' He paused. 'I feel sorry for Greg. He's a nice guy. And he hasn't had it easy.'

I thought back to what Kev had told me about his dad's drinking. In a strange way Kev and Greg had something in common. But I didn't think Kev would see it that way.

'Mark, I have to go–' I began. I knew Mum and Dad would be back any minute.

Then Mark blurted out, 'Jackie, have you seen Deirdre?'

'Er ... I've been so busy, what with Bernie, and now this with Kev,' I said uncomfortably. 'I think Deirdre's doing a lot of studying.' It didn't sound convincing, but I just couldn't tell him baldly that she was going back to Andy the Hunk.

'Tell her I was asking for her,' said Mark sadly as I hung up. Poor Mark, faithful as ever to Deirdre, who always gave him the run-around. And now there was this new Greg problem.

A high-pitched voice from the living-room reminded me that we were going to have the pleasure of Mary Rose's company for tea. Still, it might make it easier to get through the meal without it being too obvious that I had a lot on my mind.

*   *   *

'So how's *Robin Hood* coming along?' Dad asked Mary Rose with false heartiness. 'Learned all your lines yet?'

'Nah,' she giggled, with her mouth full. 'We're going to improvise.'

'Make it up as they go along,' I explained, seeing Dad's blank look.

She went on, 'So it'll be more–'

'Natural,' I muttered to Dad. I was beginning to feel like an interpreter.

'But surely it'll be chaotic if everyone just makes it up?' queried Mum, dishing out the soup.

'Teacher says it'll be great,' protested Philip. 'She says we'll have to use our imaginations.'

'Those that have any,' I put in. Mum shot me a warning look. 'Mary Rose's got the best imagination of everyone in the class,' Philip stated, glaring at me.

'Yes, that's right,' she agreed, with a modest smile. Dad put a hand to his forehead as she continued piercingly, 'I'm always imagining things. And I have lots of dreams. I tell my dreams to Phil every day.' She glanced at him tenderly. 'I could tell you about the dream I had last night about an alien who landed in my garden–'

'Maybe later,' grunted Dad. 'Better get on with your soup.'

Philip slurped his soup noisily while Mary Rose sipped dainty spoonfuls. She turned to Mum. 'This is nice soup. Is it mushroom?'

'No, it's leek and potato,' said Mum shortly. 'Philip, don't slurp.'

'My mummy makes wonderful mushroom soup,' said Mary Rose, between sips. 'My daddy says it's the best mushroom soup he's ever tasted.'

'Really?' snapped Mum. Dad looked as if he was going to throw up.

'Mary Rose is going to sing a song in the play,' said Philip. 'Go on, sing it to them, Mary Rose.'

Mary Rose didn't need any persuasion. She broke into a shrill rendering of 'You'll Never Walk Alone' with Philip watching her approvingly like a proud mother.

'How does the song fit into *Robin Hood?* I asked, when she paused for breath.

'She sings it to me when I'm lost in the forest,' said Philip. 'She finds me bawlin' crying–'

'And I sing the song and then I kiss him,' said Mary Rose. I snorted. Philip grinned sheepishly. He'd evidently become reconciled to being kissed by Mary Rose.

While Mum grilled the veggie-burgers Dad and I took bowls of salad out of the fridge and put them on the table.

Mary Rose immediately helped herself to large portions of everything. Turning to Dad with her mouth full of potato salad, she spluttered, 'My mummy and daddy can't wait to see me in the play.' Dad closed his eyes for a second and opened them again when she'd swallowed her mouthful. 'I expect you're all coming as well?' she continued. 'To see Phil?'

'Of course,' said Mum, when Dad didn't answer. 'We wouldn't dream of missing it.' She looked meaningfully at Dad.

'If they're using their imaginations,' he said, 'maybe they can imagine I'm there when I'm not.'

'No way,' said Mum frostily. 'We're all going.'

'Not me,' I said.

'*All*,' Mum repeated, with an edge to her voice.

We ate in silence for a few minutes. Then Philip

ventured, 'Lots of people are getting presents for being in the play.'

'That's right,' said Mary Rose, delicately chewing her burger. 'My mummy's buying me a silver Claddagh ring. It's very expensive.'

'Really?' grunted Dad.

'I'll probably get rollerblades,' said Philip hopefully. There was a discouraging silence.

'Did you make these burgers yourself?' Mary Rose asked Mum. 'My mummy always makes her own.'

'Well, these are vegetarian and they come from the supermarket,' Mum said sharply as she started clearing the plates. I jumped up to help with unaccustomed eagerness. Philip and Mary Rose sat there gazing fondly at each other.

'Maybe you two should go and rehearse now,' said Dad eventually, desperation in his voice.

'Yeah,' I said. 'Practice using your imaginations.'

'Please may I get down from the table?' said Mary Rose.

'Yes. Certainly.' Mum and Dad both replied together, a bit too promptly.

At the kitchen door Mary Rose said, clasping Philip's hand, 'Thank you for a lovely meal.' She grinned toothily.

When they had both thundered up the stairs Dad turned to Mum. 'When are they putting on that play?'

'Next weekend.'

'Remind me to arrange an unavoidable meeting,' Dad said to me under his breath.

'I'll be up to my eyes studying,' I said quickly. 'In fact, I'd better go up now.'

They both looked at me approvingly as I left. Guilt sat in

my stomach like a stone. I felt weighed down with Kev's secret. And I had to recognise that very soon the whole world was going to find out about it. A small voice inside me insisted that it would be better if Mum and Dad heard it from me, rather than anyone else. But maybe I could risk waiting till the case came up.

After that, all hell was going to break loose.

The Visitor

'Is it true about Kev, Jackie?' hissed Ruth as I rushed late into class the next morning. I cast her an agonised glance as I collapsed into my seat.

Deirdre sat in front of me, her soft curly hair caught back with a silver scrunchie. As soon as she turned round I could see from her expression that she knew too.

'That's your third late slip this term, Jackie,' declared Miss Kinsella.

'Sorry, Miss Kinsella,' I mumbled. 'I overslept.' She looked sceptical, but to my relief she just said, 'We're discussing the poems of Emily Dickinson.' Relieved, I opened my poetry book and stared at it, conscious of Ruth and Deirdre's eyes boring into me, waiting for the opportunity to cross-examine me about Kev.

It was going to be another heavy day, the only bonus being that school finished early on Wednesdays. But ahead lay the visit to Ballytymon with Therese, which probably wasn't going to be easy. I forced myself to focus on Emily Dickinson.

Later, in the Ballytymon bus with Deirdre, Ruth and Therese, I stared out at the golden autumn day. The leaves were just changing colour and the distant green hills, suddenly visible now the rain had stopped, were dotted with clumps of blazing yellow gorse. If only I could be up there in the peace and quiet, instead of in the centre of a noisy crowd on the bus to Ballytymon.

At break-time that morning I'd related sketchy details of Kev's action to the expectant gang. Deirdre had been annoyed at first that I hadn't confided in her. 'If you'd told me where you were going, I could have covered up for you,' she said.

'I didn't want to involve you.' I said. 'There was no point in both of us getting into trouble. Did the teacher call the roll?'

'Yeah,' said Ruth. 'But quite a few people were absent.'

After that everyone had asked me loads of questions, many of which I couldn't answer, or didn't want to, about exactly what Kev had done, and what was going to happen to him now.

Therese had pointed out in her usual brisk way how stupid Kev had been to do what he'd done, turning attention to himself, and away from the drunken driver's far worse crime. I had to agree with her about that.

As they babbled on, waves of anxiety washed over me. My mind seemed to be split between conflicting emotions. I could hear myself attempting to explain and defend what Kev had done. But, however much I tried to excuse it, I knew in my heart, like a physical pain, that what he'd done was wrong as well as stupid, and it hadn't helped anyone.

In fact, as far as his mother and Bernie were concerned, it had made everything worse.

Then to my relief the bell had rung for class, and saved me from their questions and my troubled thoughts.

*   *   *

'What's so interesting out the window, Jackie?'

Deirdre's voice penetrated my absorption, and I switched back to her and the others, sitting in the bus beside me. When they'd heard that Therese and I were going to Ballytymon to drop in on the Sinnotts, they'd decided to come along for the ride. They were going to the local shopping centre, Ruth to search for a new denim jacket just like Deirdre's, and Deirdre to make sure Ruth didn't get one exactly the same as hers.

'I've got some news too,' Ruth was announcing importantly. 'I've had the garda interview about Bernie's accident.' She waited for reactions, knowing none of the rest of us had had ours yet. 'It wasn't easy,' she went on. 'And I had a sore throat.'

'I suppose you had to go down to the station to make a statement,' said Deirdre in a weary tone, as though it was something we did all the time. 'Mine's tomorrow.'

'So's mine,' I added. Ruth looked annoyed at the interruption.

I took pity on her. 'What did they ask you?'

'Well, first they asked my name, age and address,' began Ruth. Deirdre caught my eye. We were obviously going to get a blow-by-blow account.

'Get to the point, Ruth,' snapped Therese. Ruth glared at

her. 'They said I was very helpful,' she said, in injured tones.

'Did you go down there on your own?' I asked hastily.

'No, my dad came,' she said. 'There was this really cool woman garda. She looked like someone out of "NYPD Blue".'

'What did they actually ask?' said Deirdre impatiently.

'There were lots of questions about where we were when the accident happened, what time it was, what we heard—'

'Could you remember everything?' asked Therese.

'Well, some of it,' said Ruth. 'They wanted to know how fast the car was going, but I told them we didn't see that. Then they asked what we found when we got to the scene.'

That silenced everyone. None of us was ever likely to forget that scene. We all looked out of the window, trying not to remember.

*   *   *

Therese and I could hear the Sinnotts' doorbell echoing through the house as we tried it for the third time.

'They must be back staying at their aunt's,' said Therese as we started walking down the path. From previous visits my memories of the small front garden were of a neat lawn and blooming roses. Now the hedges were untrimmed and a battered football and a couple of children's toys lay abandoned in the overgrown grass.

We were nearly back at the front gate when we heard a chain rattling as the door was opened. Turning, I saw Mrs

Sinnott in the doorway clutching a worn dressing-gown round her thin body. She motioned us to come in and, as we approached, I saw that she had huge dark shadows under her eyes and her face was drained of colour.

'We're really sorry to disturb you,' I said, shocked at her appearance. At the hospital with Bernie she'd looked very stressed, but never as bad as this.

'It's all right,' she said with a wan smile. 'It's so good of you both to come. Please come in.'

In the kitchen Therese and I exchanged worried glances as Mrs Sinnott went to put the kettle on. 'Honestly, don't bother with tea,' said Therese. 'We only came to see if we could do anything to help.'

'With the kids and stuff,' I added.

'They've gone to their auntie's,' said Mrs Sinnott. 'I'm only just out of hospital myself.' Her voice was weak. 'I was hoping to get in to see Bernie later.' She tried to pour the tea but her hand was trembling so much that Therese took it from her and poured out three cups.

'I saw Bernie yesterday,' I told her. 'She's out of the intensive care now. And I think she can see better.' I didn't mention any of Bernie's other problems, her hesitant speech, her memory loss, her agitation, her pain.

'You're such a good friend to her,' said Mrs Sinnott. She turned to Therese. 'All of you.' She lifted her cup in her shaking hand, and then carefully put it down again as if it was too heavy for her slender wrist. 'We've had more problems in the family, you know.' Two tears oozed out and trickled down her cheeks. I looked at Therese.

'My son got into trouble,' she went on. 'He was so angry

and upset about his sister.'

'I know,' I whispered.

'He's such a good boy,' she said, seemingly oblivious of the tears rolling down her cheeks. 'He's just had so much to cope with. I'm afraid I'm not much help to him.' She attempted a smile which turned into a sort of grimace. 'Or to any of them. Bernie kept us all going, and now without her, everything's going wrong.'

I wanted to say something comforting, but I couldn't find the right words. While I was still deliberating, Therese declared in her confident way, 'Don't worry, Mrs Sinnott. Bernie's getting better, and maybe things won't go too badly for Kev.'

'Of course,' said Mrs Sinnott, straightening up a little. 'You're right. If I could just feel a bit more on top of things ...'

'Is there anything we can do?' I asked. I knew it was a useless question, but what else could you say?

'You've been a help already,' said Mrs Sinnott, and she smiled the old sweet smile that I remembered. 'You've both cheered me up.'

There was a ring at the doorbell. Maybe it was Kev. Although I knew he wasn't usually home this early, my heart jumped at the possibility.

'It must be my neighbour,' said Mrs Sinnott.

'Shall I get it?' I asked.

'Oh, would you?' she said gratefully. 'I look such a mess.'

I opened the door. Before me stood a vision. A tall strik-ing girl, tanned, with cropped peroxide hair and huge blue eyes with long curling lashes. She was wearing an expensive-looking leather jacket, tight check trousers and strappy high-heeled sandals, and she was carrying a back-pack covered with little flags.

'Is this the home of Andy?' she said, in a strong German accent.

'Andy?' I repeated, puzzled. The only Andy I knew was Andy the Hunk.

'I think Andy Byrne is his full name,' she said carefully. 'But maybe it is his friend Kevin who lives here. I have both addresses here and I do not know which is which.'

I stared at her, speechless. 'It is Andy for whom I am searching,' she added, running her fingers through her hair. I caught sight of a gleaming watch with masses of dials and figures on it, and lots of rings.

'And you are–' I said faintly.

'I am from Germany,' she said. 'I am Monika.'

The Mirror

BERNIE

When Bernie woke in the early morning, there was always an instant of tranquillity before she became aware of all the inexplicable things that had changed in her life. For that blessed few seconds, she thought she was at home, about to do all the usual morning chores before school.

Then pain, confusion and bewilderment flooded back, and she knew she was in this new strange place where people kept speaking to her as if she was a child, asking her things, misunderstanding what she tried to say, poking needles into her.

'Good morning, Bernie,' said the woman in the opposite bed. 'How're you feeling today?' Bernie didn't have the energy yet to try and find the right words to reply, so she just nodded.

The nurse came to help her eat her breakfast. Even her good hand didn't have the strength to hold the spoon steady. Then they manoeuvred her out of bed, a slow and painful process. 'You're getting stronger, dear,' encouraged the nurse, as Bernie staggered, clutching on to her for dear life, and collapsed into the armchair beside the bed.

At lunch-time the nurse from the intensive care appeared. 'I'm just going off duty,' she said cheerily. 'I'm knackered.'

Bernie smiled. 'Tired,' she said.

'Well done!' said the nurse. 'And now, can you remember my name? I told you again yesterday.'

Bernie remembered the nurse's visit, but as usual, the name escaped her. She shook her head sadly. 'Never mind,' said the nurse. 'You're coming along very well. Don't you worry about a thing.'

The woman opposite said to the nurse, 'Did you know she's got an admirer?'

'Has she?' said the nurse.

'There's a red-headed young man who comes in every day,' said the woman. 'And he brings her flowers.' She indicated the yellow chrysanthemums on Bernie's locker.

Later, after she'd done her daily exercises and had her dressings changed, she saw the woman in the opposite bed peering into a little mirror as she applied make-up and lipstick. Noticing Bernie watching her she asked, 'Would you like me to put some on for you? A bit of make-up is great for your morale.' When Bernie didn't reply she came over and held out the powder compact.

Bernie took it and peered into the mirror. She gave a little whimper. A strange face stared back at her. The head, almost bald except for a few tiny golden tufts of hair, was partially covered by a large dressing. The face was thin, discoloured with bruises, the eyes were enormous and one of them was bloodshot. Who was this person? It couldn't be

her, Bernie. But she knew it was. She flung the mirror away
from her.

Through her sobs she heard the glass shatter. People hurried over to her, talking, talking. She buried her face in the
pillow and cried as if her heart was breaking.

*   *   *

'How long have you been in Ireland, Monika?' asked Mrs Sinnott politely as we sat awkwardly round the kitchen table.

'Indeed, I have only yesterday come,' said Monika, her
smile showing a set of perfect teeth. I wondered whether
they were naturally perfect, or whether she had spent
years wearing braces like the rest of us.

'I am coming here to improve my English,' she continued.

'It's very good already,' said Mrs Sinnott.

'Where are you staying?' asked Therese. We were both
staring at Monika, afraid to catch each other's eye in case
we burst into giggles.

'I am just now in a guest-house,' answered Monika. She
waved a slender hand tipped with long purple nails. I
counted six silver rings. 'But Andy, he tells me to come to
stay with him if I come to Ireland.'

'Er, does he know you're coming?' I asked.

'I write to him, but I did not receive any reply,' she said.
'Perhaps there is a delay with the post?'

'Sometimes there is,' said Mrs Sinnott. She rose from the
table. 'I have to go and lie down,' she said. 'I haven't been
feeling well,' she explained to Monika, 'and I need to rest
now so that I can go and visit my daughter in hospital this

evening. You'll have to excuse me.'

Monika nodded sympathetically. 'I am sorry.'

'Maybe you girls wouldn't mind waiting till Kev gets back?' Mrs Sinnott said to Therese and me. 'He won't be long. Then he can bring Monika to Andy's.' She left the kitchen and we could hear her halting footsteps dragging up the stairs.

'The poor lady is not well, I can see,' said Monika.

There was a silence. Then Therese said, 'Would you like a cold drink or anything? I don't know what there is in the fridge. We're just visiting.'

'I understand,' said Monika. 'I would very much like a glass of water.'

I found a glass beside the sink and filled it with water from the tap. Monika looked surprised. 'It is safe to drink this?' she asked. 'In my country we drink only mineral water.'

'Well, we've been drinking it for years and it hasn't done us any harm,' retorted Therese.

'Ach, that is fine with me,' said Monika. 'It is only that now there are so much things we must be careful, for the environment you know, chemicals and colourings—'

'And aerosol sprays because of the ozone layer,' I put in. 'You must meet our friend Ruth, you'd have a lot in common.'

'I would very much like this,' said Monika eagerly. 'You are all friends of Andy, no?'

'Not quite,' said Therese. She looked at me. 'Kev is, of course.'

And so is Deirdre, I added silently, though I don't think she's going to be for much longer.

*   *   *

BERNIE

Bernie was dozing after the upset of the afternoon. Following her outburst the ward sister and the nurses had bustled around her and the doctor had appeared.

Everyone had assured her that she was on the mend, her hair was starting to grow again, her collar-bone was healing, the bruises would fade, her memory was returning, and she would soon be able to speak normally.

Bernie nodded in agreement, and even managed to smile at the woman whose mirror she had broken, who had approached her, full of remorse at her own thoughtlessness.

But there was a false ring to their reassurances, and Bernie wondered how true any of it was, or if they were just saying these things to make her feel better.

'Bernie?'

She opened her eyes. It was him, the fella with the red hair who brought her the flowers. He was carrying a little package. 'I brought this for you.'

He watched her fumbling with the paper. Then he gently took it from her and unwrapped it. It was a perfume spray. She smiled in delight as he carefully sprayed her good wrist. The sweet heady scent wafted upwards and filled her nostrils, accustomed for so long to the hospital mixture of stuffy air, food-smells and antiseptic.

'Thank you.' To her relief it came out sounding normal. Encouraged, she continued, 'Who ... you are?' It wasn't quite right, but he'd understood.

For a few moments he said nothing, a strained expression on his kind freckled face. Then he said slowly, 'I told you my name, Greg.'

She nodded. 'But–'

'Let's just say I'm really sorry about your accident,' he said quickly. 'And I'd like to help you get better.' He smiled at her anxiously, like a small child who badly wanted something and was afraid of being refused.

She reached out with her good hand and picked up the perfume. 'It's ... lovely,' she said. 'It's a nice ... smell.'

Joy surged through her as she realised that she'd found the right words, and spoken them, loud and clear.

*　　　　*　　　　*

Kev's face was a picture when he entered the kitchen of his house and found us all sitting there. His bewildered glance jumped first to me, then Therese, and last of all, Monika. He stayed focused on her, speechless. Eventually he said uncertainly, 'Monika?'

'Ach Kevin, it is wonderful to see you again. *Céad Míle Fáilte!*' and she shook his hand enthusiastically. Looking round at our astonished expressions she added with a laugh, 'It is Irish, no? What Andy was teaching me?'

Kev scratched his head. 'Could someone tell me what's going on?'

*　　　　*　　　　*

When everything had been explained to Kev, and we'd shared a Coke and some biscuits he'd found, Therese said to Kev, 'We're coming with you to Andy's.'

'I don't think–' he began.

'Oh, no,' Therese interrupted. '*This*, we're not going to

miss.' She muttered to me, 'Pity Deirdre's not here to see Andy lost for words for once in his life.'

Kev grinned, brushing aside the lock of fair hair that always fell over his forehead. The melting feeling began inside me, even though Therese and Monika were watching. It was so great to see him looking happy again, even for a moment.

'Ach, I see that Jackie is still the girl-friend of Kevin,' said Monika, beaming at us. I was getting to quite like her.

'That's enough of all this stuff,' said Therese sharply. 'Let's get to Andy's. I just hope he's there.'

*   *   *

Andy was there. He opened the door himself, wearing head-phones and his Phonics T-shirt. Like Kev, his eyes swivelled over the whole bunch of us, finally resting on Monika. His mouth opened, but no sound emerged. He looked like a fish on a hook, gasping for air. And in a way, I thought, that's what he was. Caught!

Monika rushed forward and flung her arms around him, crooning what sounded like endearments in German. Then she switched to English. 'My dear Andy, we are at last together! So long I have been waiting to see you again!'

'So have I,' I whispered to Therese.

Andy stood like a zombie. We could hear a tinny version of All Saints coming from his head-phones, displaced by Monika's violent hug. He looked round wildly, and his eyes fell on Monika's backpack. He put his hand to his head and muttered, 'Oh no.'

'Poor Andy,' cooed Monika, nuzzling his neck. 'Did you not get my letter? You are, what is the word you have taught me jah, *gobsmacked.*'

Andy found his voice. 'Yeah,' he said. 'That's exactly what I am ... gobsmacked.'

The Lawyer

Kev and I walked to the bus stop, arm in arm. We'd left Monika with a shell-shocked Andy.

'Andy has told me about his very good friends,' Monika had said as we left. 'I hope we will all go out together soon. But, of course, Andy must work hard to be a pilot, so he will not have so much time.' Andy looked sick.

'A pilot?' snorted Therese. 'Oh yeah, he'll fly you to wherever you want to go, Monika. He's especially good at stunts.'

'Thanks, Therese,' said Andy wryly. 'You're a great help.'

'What shall we tell Deirdre, Andy?' asked Therese mockingly. Our last sight as the front door slammed shut was of Andy standing in the hall with Monika draped around him.

When Therese had veered off to her house, still laughing, Kev said, 'Poor old Andy. His sins have followed him home.'

'At least now Deirdre'll see him in his true colours,' I said. 'Then I s'pose it'll be back to Mark, as per usual.'

We walked without speaking for a bit, past front gardens bright with late roses. It had begun to drizzle rain again, and a rich damp smell rose up from the moist earth. Kev's arm around me made me feel safe and secure, though I knew we were still beset by troubles.

'Have you seen the lawyer yet?' I asked him.

'I went in with my uncle this morning,' he said. 'The lawyer says that now that I've pleaded guilty, my best chance is to apologise to the judge and to the Gilmartins, and admit what I did was wrong.'

'If you do that, and they understand why you did it, what's the worst that could happen?'

'It depends on the judge,' said Kev gloomily. 'The lawyer keeps saying they don't like people taking the law into their own hands. He's hoping I'll only get a probation order. I'd have to undertake not to get in any more trouble, and I might have to pay compensation.' He paused, and added in a low voice, 'But because I've turned seventeen I could be sent to St Patrick's.' In spite of the mildness of the evening I shivered.

Kev must have felt the tremor, because he stopped and tightened his arm, swinging me round to face him. 'Look, I'll apologise if I have to, but nothing will make me stop hating Gilmartin.' His tone was savage.

I thought, how long before he finds out that Gilmartin's son knows Mark? Kev might try and attack the son again. And in a way, after what Mark had told me, I had begun to feel sorry for Greg Gilmartin. What his father had done wasn't Greg's fault. He hadn't even known about it till Mark told him.

Kev let go of me, and we walked on without touching. I wanted to take his hand, but he looked so forbidding. 'There's a probation officer coming to our house tomorrow,' he went on, 'a kind of social worker sent by the court.' He scowled. 'These people really piss me off. They'll never understand.'

'Kev,' I argued. 'They're trying to help you.' Though I figured that with his present attitude, they weren't going to get very far.

'I slipped in to see Bernie on my way home,' he said, his grim expression softening. 'She was a bit brighter, though they said she was upset earlier on. Did you bring her the flowers and that perfume?'

'Perfume?' I said, puzzled. 'No. I saw the flowers yesterday, I thought your aunt or someone brought them.'

Kev frowned. 'Maybe it was one of the nurses,' I suggested.

'There was coloured wrapping paper, as though someone had brought them in for her,' he said.

'Probably a neighbour.'

'I don't think so,' he said. 'There aren't many visitors. She kept saying something about a fella, but it wasn't very clear.'

'She tried to tell me about a fella too,' I told him.

'It's desperate the way she can't talk properly,' he muttered. 'The doctors say it'll get better, but I wonder.'

We passed a large building set back from the road in its own grounds.

'Isn't that Bernie's school, where we came for the disco last year?' I asked Kev.

He didn't answer, and I guessed he was thinking, like I

was, about Bernie lying in hospital instead having a normal day at school like everyone else, and of the reason why.

'I know,' I said suddenly. 'It might've been her teacher, Mr Russell, who brought those things for Bernie!'

'Yeah,' said Kev. 'I s'pose it could've been him.' We reached the bus stop and huddled under the shelter as the rain started again. 'Decent guy, that teacher,' added Kev.

*   *   *

'It's Wednesday,' said Mum sharply when I got home. 'You're usually home early.' I sensed trouble.

'Mm,' I mumbled, 'but I had to go to Ballytymon with Therese.'

'Why?'

'We went to see Bernie's ma,' I answered reluctantly.

'Oh really!' Mum exploded. 'First you're running to the hospital all the time to see Bernie—'

'Come on, Mum, we've been over that,' I said as quietly as I could.

'I know,' she said. 'You made your point about that, and we accepted it. But I don't see why you have to go out to Ballytymon as well, when you should be studying.'

I couldn't even begin to explain about Kev and Mrs Sinnott, and all their problems, and how much they needed support. 'Well, I'm back now,' I said mildly, 'and I'm going upstairs to study.' And I trudged upstairs, dragging my bag behind me.

Mum sighed, and went in to finish watching 'Open House'.

I couldn't handle a row just now. I knew there was going be the mother of all battles when they found out about Kev.

*   *   *

After tea that evening, trying to write an essay on the 'Causes of the First World War', I wondered whether Deirdre and Ruth had got back from shopping. As though there wasn't enough hassle around already, I was now going to have to break the news to Deirdre about the arrival of Monika.

I had never thought Deirdre really cared about Andy the way I did about Kev. But her pride was going to be hurt, and Deirdre wasn't going to take kindly to that. On the other hand, it was going to be good news for Mark.

I heard the doorbell ring, and then light footsteps come up the stairs. Definitely not Philip's thundering tread.

My door opened and Deirdre appeared. 'Success!' she said, closing the door behind her. 'We actually found a denim jacket in Miss Selfridge that Ruth liked, and that looked okay. We went into fourteen shops first.' She flung herself on to my bed. 'I'm wrecked!'

'Great,' I said. My half-hearted response registered immediately.

'What's wrong, Jackie?' I nearly laughed. What was wrong? My whole life had turned into one big mess, and Deirdre wanted to know what was wrong. I hoped she'd realise that compared to everything else that was happening, Andy's crime was a minor one.

'Well,' I began, 'it's about Andy.'

The Name

I t was Saturday. At last I could draw a breath after one of
the most stressful weeks of my life. I lay in bed trying to
get myself moving.

From the garden I could hear the buzz of the lawn-
mower as Dad cut the grass. There were sounds of activity
from Philip's room as Mum helped him get his stuff ready
for the school play.

The play! I realised with horror it must be tonight. I'd
forgotten all about it. And Mum had made it clear that there
was no way Dad or I would be let off. Gran and Nana had
been roped in too, but unlike us, they were probably going
to enjoy it.

But I'd agreed to go with Deirdre to see Bernie at the
evening visiting time. Kev had said he'd meet us at the hospital, and that he'd fill me in on how he'd got on with the
social worker.

Now I'd have to try and go this afternoon instead. I'd
better get up and ring Deirdre. As I yawned, and slowly
pulled back the duvet, my mind went spinning back to the

other night, when I'd told Deirdre about Andy's unexpected visitor.

'The cow!' Deirdre had spat out, when I started to tell her the story.

'Monika's not a cow!' I'd protested. 'She's actually quite nice. Andy's the one who's been two-timing both of you, and telling lies all round.' I couldn't resist adding, 'I told you he wasn't to be trusted.'

'Well, of course,' she said defensively, 'I always knew I couldn't really rely on him'

'Not like Mark,' I put in.

Deirdre lolled back on my bed. 'It's just that Andy was more fun. And so gorgeous.' She sighed. 'Even if he was a lying, two-faced git.'

I noticed with approval that she was using the past tense.

*   *   *

BERNIE

Bernie watched her ma coming into the ward. She was carrying a bag which Bernie knew contained fresh night-clothes and underwear for her. Now she could see more clearly, she noticed how frail her mother looked. Strain and exhaustion showed in her face, under the smile she knew her ma put on for her benefit.

'How are you today, love?' her ma said.

Today was a good day, and Bernie managed to say, 'Feel ... lot better.' Her mother busied herself putting things away in the locker. She picked up the perfume and sprayed Bernie's temples. Bernie sniffed appreciatively.

'Whoever brought you this was very thoughful,' said Mrs Sinnott. 'I suppose it was one of your friends?' Bernie shook her head.

But she knew it was useless trying to explain about the fella with red hair, who came nearly every day, and spoke to her so gently. He talked about school and his computer, and the music he liked. He said he was going to bring her a tape of some band, but she'd forgotten the name.

Sometimes he looked quite sad. He talked about some of the problems he had at home, and she had flashes of memory about similar problems in her own home, a place that seemed so remote now that she sometimes wondered if it still existed.

Bernie could rarely find the words to tell the fella she understood how he felt. But she knew he sensed her sympathy. Once he took her hand and held it for a while. She'd liked that ...

'The girls send their love,' her ma was saying. 'They're having a great time at Joan's. Everyone's making a big fuss of them.' Her voice had a kind of false cheerfulness.

'Are you–' Bernie summoned her strength. 'Are you ... sure?'

'Oh yes,' her ma said. 'They're fine.'

It had come out wrong again. Bernie'd wanted to ask if her ma was sure she herself was okay. She looked so pale and tired.

The cheerful nurse from the intensive care appeared. Bernie knew what she was going to ask. She had made an enormous effort to keep repeating the nurse's name to herself every little while.

'What's my name, Bernie?' said the nurse, as usual.

Her mother and the nurse waited. Bernie shut her eyes. Her whole body tensed. Seconds passed. The trolley with the lunches appeared.

'Don't worry, Bernie–' the nurse began. Mrs Sinnott rose to help Bernie with her lunch.

'Moon,' Bernie almost shouted. 'Something to do with ... moon.'

They both stared. Then the nurse let out a whoop. 'You're right!' she cried. 'It's Mooney! I'm Nurse Helen Mooney!' And she planted a kiss on Bernie's cheek.

Bernie looked at her mother, standing beside the bed with a bowl of soup in her hand. She saw that there were tears in her eyes.

The Confrontation

When Deirdre and I got to the hospital that Saturday afternoon the curtains were drawn round Bernie's bed.

'She's asleep,' said the nurse in reply to our anxious queries. 'There was a bit of excitement this morning.' And she told us how it had become clear that Bernie's memory was improving. 'Though she still has speech and movement difficulties, of course, and she gets very tired,' she added. 'Why don't you pop into the waiting-room till she wakes? There's a drinks machine and a telly there.'

*　　　　*　　　　*

'I wonder how Monika is getting on in Andy's?' Sitting in uncomfortable shiny brown armchairs in the hospital waiting-room, Deirdre and I were going over the Andy-Monika saga for the zillionth time. By now, Deirdre's anger had faded, and she'd even got to the point of being able to laugh about it.

'D'you think he's broken it to her that he's not about to

become a pilot?' I said. We laughed.

'Mind you,' said Deirdre unexpectedly, 'he's really keen on planes. Maybe he will become a pilot some day.' So in spite of everything, I reflected, she still had a soft spot for him.

'I'd like to see Monika again,' I said. 'Maybe we could ask her round when things have calmed down.' If they ever do, I added silently.

Deirdre picked up a magazine and turned to 'Your Stars'. '*"In the early part of the month the conjunction of planets will lead to changes in your life,"*' she read aloud. '*"An opportunity to travel could arise, and a possible career change."* And listen to this. *"Though old relationships may be coming to an end, this is the time for a new start and an exciting new relationship."*' She looked at me triumphantly.

'That reminds me,' I said. 'Have you seen Mark?' Not quite an exciting new relationship, I thought, but it would have to do.

'Well, I went over to his house to tell him how useful those history notes were,' she admitted. The ones she'd rubbished at the time, I recalled. 'He showed me how to send e-mail on his computer,' she continued. 'It's cool.'

'Maybe that could be the career change,' I suggested. 'Computers.'

I hoped there hadn't been any e-mail from Greg while she was there. Fortunately it appeared that Mark and Deirdre's resuming relationship was taking priority over everything else.

Kev appeared in the doorway. 'Hi,' he said. 'What're you

doing in here? Is Bernie okay?'

We repeated what the nurse had said. 'She should be awake soon,' I told him.

'Fine,' he said, sitting beside me. He was wearing the blue sweatshirt that I liked, and he appeared less tense and more relaxed than I'd seen him for ages. Maybe the session with the probation officer hadn't gone so badly.

Sizing up the situation, Deirdre said, 'I'll just go and see if Bernie's awake yet.' As she left the room she shot me a meaningful look, in case I hadn't fully appreciated her tact in leaving us alone. I just wished Kev and I were being left alone to talk about something more romantic than Kev's interview with the probation officer.

*   *   *

'How'd it go?' I asked Kev.

'Could've been worse,' he said. He stretched out his long body in the armchair and clasped his hands behind his head. 'She wasn't a bit like I expected, young, wearing jeans,' he went on. 'She told us to call her Kathy. My ma made tea, and we sat round the kitchen table.'

'Was anyone else there?' I asked

'My uncle,' he said. 'And Joan brought the kids round for a bit. Kathy wanted to meet them.'

'What did she ask you?'

'She wanted to know about everything,' he said. 'About my dad going off, what it was like before he went, and my ma's nerves. She asked about how we'd all got on in school, and how we managed on social welfare.'

'What about Bernie and the accident?' I asked.

His face darkened. 'I went into her office the next day and saw her on my own,' he said. 'I gave her the whole story. What bleeding Gilmartin did to Bernie, and how he just carried on with *his* life while Bernie's life was wrecked, and all our lives with it.' His voice trembled. 'I told her how I felt, how I had to do something to show him, to frighten him, to make him realise what he'd done.'

For a moment neither of us spoke. I put my hand on Kev's, where it rested in his lap. He turned his hand and held mine in both of his. 'I told her about you,' he said.

'Me?'

He gave a little strained smile. 'She asked if I had a girl-friend.' Hearing him say that word made my heart leap. 'I said you'd tried to stop me doing anything stupid.'

'What did she say?'

'She said I was lucky to have such a sensible girlfriend,' he said quietly. 'She said I should have listened to you.' He leaned forward and looked at me directly, his grey eyes serious. 'She was right. What I did just made everything worse. I know that now. But I couldn't help it.'

We sat there in the bare waiting-room holding hands until Deirdre came back to tell us Bernie was awake and waiting for us.

*   *   *

Half an hour later we came out of Ward B7, chatting as we walked along the corridor.

'She's a lot better than when I last saw her—' Deirdre was saying. As she spoke I noticed a figure approaching from the other end of the corridor. I glanced at him as he drew nearer. He was about our age, carrying a bunch of flowers. Such flaming red hair, I thought idly.

Kev suddenly went rigid. Deirdre looked at him. 'What's wrong, Kev?' she asked. 'Forgotten something?'

The guy with red hair was close to us now. His freckled face flushed as his eyes met Kev's. 'I'm sorry,' he began. 'I didn't—'

Kev turned white. 'Get out of here,' he said, very deliberately. 'Keep away from my sister.' The guy took a step backwards.

Everything suddenly became clear. The flowers, the perfume, the 'fella' that Bernie had talked about. I tried to grab Kev, but he evaded me and lunged towards the guy.

'Who is he?' Deirdre shouted as she looked down at them struggling on the floor of the corridor. People started running towards them. A blue-coated porter tried to separate them.

'His name is Greg,' I said. I was trembling. 'Greg Gilmartin.'

The Play

We sat in a row in the darkened hall of Philip's school, listening to two kids from sixth class murdering a violin and piano duet.

'Good thing Beethoven isn't around to hear what's being done to his music,' whispered Dad.

'I think Beethoven was deaf himself, dear, actually,' said Gran loudly.

'Just as well,' said Dad.

'*Shh!*' Mum frowned over at us.

'Donal's teacher told us that he definitely shows promise,' I heard a mother say. 'He just needs practice.'

'You can say that again,' Dad said. To shut Dad up, Mum passed round a packet of Softmints and we all started chewing.

'My teeth,' hissed Nana from her seat beside Mum. 'These mints are sticking in my teeth.' Mum gave an audible sigh. 'And my head's still throbbing from that percussion band,' Nana continued. 'Why in the world they have to have amplification, I don't know.'

'Shh, it's the Irish dancing now,' said Mum, as a bunch of little kids rushed on and started clattering away to the fiddle music.

'Call that Irish dancing?' said a father sitting nearby. 'That's just leppin' about. In my day–'

'"Riverdance" they're not,' agreed Dad.

'Doesn't little Aisling look a doat in her costume?' whispered a proud grandfather.

'I can't get that mint out of my teeth,' muttered Nana.

*   *   *

I had got home from the hospital with three minutes to spare before we had to leave for Philip's school. Luckily Mum, Nana and Gran had been too busy trying to soothe Philip's nerves and sort out his costume to notice my lateness, but I was aware of Dad throwing me a funny look when I came in. I wondered if the recent drama at the hospital had somehow left a visible mark on me.

I'd watched in horror as Kev and Greg struggled on the floor of the hospital corridor, like a scene in a film. The porter eventually pulled them apart, and the ward sister appeared, her face like thunder. 'What do you think you're doing?' she stormed. 'This is a hospital, not a circus. I've a good mind to call the police.'

Oh no, I thought. If Kev's in more trouble with the gardaí before the other case is even heard, he'll be finished.

The porter indicated Kev. 'It was that lad started it,' he said. 'He jumped on this fella here.'

Greg's flowers were strewn all over the floor. He was

mopping ineffectually at the blood which trickled from his nose. Kev was breathing heavily, his sweatshirt ripped at the sleeve.

Deirdre and I stood among a circle of people who had gathered, neither of us knowing what to say or do. This is all like some kind of nightmare, I thought, finding myself involved in one disaster after another, and being powerless to prevent them.

The ward sister looked more closely at Kev. 'Aren't you the brother of the patient in my ward?' she asked. 'Bernie Sinnott?' He nodded.

'And this other lad is a pal of hers too,' volunteered another nurse. 'He often comes to visit her.'

'He's no friend of hers,' Kev hissed.

'Isn't he her boyfriend?' asked the nurse.

I could see Kev gritting his teeth. 'No,' I said quickly. 'It was his father who knocked Bernie down and nearly killed her!'

'Well, I'm not having my patients upset by this kind of disturbance,' declared the sister. She turned to Greg. 'If this boy attacked you, I'm quite prepared to call the gardaí,' she told him. Delving into the pocket of her uniform, she handed him a wad of cotton wool which he held to his bloody nose.

'No,' said Greg, in a low voice. He had a soft Cork accent. 'There's no need to call the gardaí. I'm okay.' He looked at Kev. 'Let's forget it.' And he bent down and started gathering the ruined flowers from the floor.

It was such a pathetic sight that I had to resist the urge to help him. But I knew Kev would never forgive me if I did.

The sister glared at Kev. 'If you ever–' she began. But like the answer to a prayer a familiar voice said, 'What's going on here?' It was Mr Russell, evidently on his way to see Bernie. I was never so relieved to see anyone.

Everyone started explaining everything to Mr Russell, except Greg, still picking up his flowers, and Kev, angry defiance written all over him.

In the end Deirdre took over and told Mr Russell what had happened. He was pretty quick on the uptake. Turning to the furious ward sister, he said soothingly, 'It's all right, Sister, I'm Bernie's teacher. Leave it to me. I'll deal with these lads.'

She looked mollified. 'My patient comes first,' she said. 'I don't want her upset. She'd better not hear about any of this.'

'We'll make sure of that,' said Mr Russell. 'I'm really sorry this happened.' He added, 'Both these lads have had a tough time lately.' And he put an arm each round a reluctant Kev and Greg and shepherded them into a nearby waiting-room, indicating to Deirdre and me to follow.

*   *   *

'Philip's on,' whispered Gran excitedly, jerking me out of my trance.

On the makeshift stage a teacher was announcing, 'And now, our improvised play by fifth and sixth class. Ladies and gentlemen, *Robin Hood*, with a difference!'

There was loud applause from our row, and some from the other side of the hall where I guessed Mary Rose's mummy and daddy were sitting.

Then Philip's friend Conor strolled on to the stage in front of the curtains, chewing as usual, and holding a hand-written sign upside down. People craned their necks. 'Sherwood Forest,' everyone whispered to each other. Conor strolled off again, still chewing.

'Isn't that the boy who's Philip's friend?' asked Nana loudly. 'How can he act and chew at the same time?'

'Well, he hasn't said anything so far,' Dad pointed out.

The curtains swung back to reveal several kids in brown tunics, their outstretched arms entwined with green leaves. 'They're trees,' everyone chorused. There was a long pause. Then Philip, in his tissue paper skirt and flowery hat, round spots of rouge on each cheek, clumped on in his Doc Martens.

'Those shoes don't do much for the outfit,' said Mum under her breath. 'I knew we should have tried to find the ballet shoes.'

Philip addressed the audience in a falsetto voice. 'I'm lost in the forest. It's really dangerous on account of me bein' a girl. There could be gangs of criminals or mad cows or something.' He sat on the ground and let out a deafening howl. Nana jumped.

There was another long pause. Then Mary Rose appeared in her green tights, wearing knee-high leather boots and a green and white baseball cap turned the wrong way round. She was clinging on to the shoulders of a hefty boy, obviously supposed to be her horse.

He collapsed in mid-gallop, shedding her on to the floor with a thump. A voice from the audience called, 'Are you all right, Mary Rose, poppet?'

Mary Rose jumped up beaming toothily from ear to ear. 'I'm okay, Mummy,' she piped. She ran on tiptoe to Philip and said in a deep voice. 'Do not cry, Maid Marian. I, Robin, am here to save you from the mad cows an' all.'

A sheepish crowd of kids in green tights were pushed on reluctantly from the side of the stage. They were all carrying toy bows and arrows. 'We're the Merry Men,' they mumbled half-heartedly. 'We rob rich people to help the poor.'

Mary Rose scampered over to them. 'Ho, Merry Men,' she boomed. 'We must be careful of the Sheriff of Nottingham. He's after me and my friends, Friar Tuck and–' she paused. 'The other one, little somebody.'

'John,' called her mother.

Philip meanwhile appeared to be getting fed up. He plodded over to Mary Rose and looked up at her. 'Help me find my father, Robin,' he squeaked. 'He'll be raging if I'm late home from the forest.'

She patted his shoulder reassuringly. 'I just have to sing this song.' And she burst in to her familiar rendering of 'You'll Never Walk Alone'. Her mother joined in the chorus from her seat.

'Not again,' sighed Dad. To my amazement Gran, Nana and Mum were all joining in enthusiastically, and so was the rest of the audience. At the end Mary Rose pranced over to Philip, whipped off her glasses, and gave him a loud smacking kiss on his cheek. The audience cheered.

'Oh well done, darling,' commented the well-bred voice of Mary Rose's mother. Philip stood bashfully wiping his cheek with the back of his hand, smudging the circle of rouge. It gave him a peculiar one-sided blush.

The Merry Men milled about on the stage. 'What're we s'posed to do now?' asked one.

'You've to act merry,' said Mary Rose in a stage whisper. A couple of them started skipping about obediently.

'Now, Maid Marian,' shouted Mary Rose enthusiastically, 'I will help you find your father.'

There was a silence. 'It's getting dark,' prompted a teacher's voice from backstage.

'Oh yeah, it's getting dark,' repeated Philip. 'We'll have to let him know where I am, or he'll kill me when I get home.'

Mary Rose thought hard. 'I know what to do,' she announced to Philip and the audience. 'We'll send him a fax.'

The Peace

Just as well everyone in the house was still in bed recovering from Philip's play, I thought. It was the next morning, and Ruth was waiting impatiently at the other end of the phone to hear the news.

'What happened after Mr Russell stopped the fight?' she asked.

'Well, we were all in the waiting-room,' I told her. 'Mr Russell shut the door so no-one would come in. Then he made us all sit down.'

'Yeah?' prompted Ruth.

I thought back to the scene. Greg was still holding the blood-stained cotton wool to his nose with one hand and clutching the drooping flowers in their torn paper in the other. Kev had slumped into a chair, refusing to look at Greg.

'Now listen,' said Mr Russell. He spoke quietly, but there was an authority in his tone that I hadn't heard before. 'Kev, your mother has told me what your family has been through and I sympathise. But you're not a child.

Lashing out wildly like you did last week, and again just now, is not the answer. Last week's effort has brought you to court, and given your ma more worry and anxiety, as though she hasn't had enough.'

Kev started to speak, but Mr Russell raised his hand. 'I haven't finished.' Kev subsided. 'And as for today, starting a fight in a hospital where your own sister is being cared for–'

'He shouldn't have come here,' said Kev. 'Then it wouldn't have happened.' But he sounded subdued.

Greg cleared his throat nervously and looked away from Kev towards Deirdre and me. 'I didn't mean to cause any more trouble,' he stammered. 'I feel so bad about what happened to Bernie. I just wanted to try and help her, after what my dad–' He stopped, looking down at the flowers in his hand.

'Kev, I know you're a good lad, and you care about your mother and your sister,' said Mr Russell after a moment. 'I want you to answer this question honestly.' He paused.

Kev said nothing.

'Look at Greg,' Mr Russell commanded. Reluctantly, Kev raised his eyes. Greg's forehead was damp with sweat, but he didn't avoid Kev's glance.

Mr Russell continued, 'Is Greg in any way to blame for what happened to Bernie?'

There was a long silence. Deirdre and I sat there like the audience at a particularly dramatic play. We could hear distant voices and trolleys clattering outside in the corridor. The tension in the room was almost tangible.

Kev drew a deep breath. Then he said slowly, 'No, I

suppose it's not really his fault.' And he looked over at me, as though there was no-one else in the room.

*   *   *

'It's like an episode of 'ER',' said Ruth over the phone, as I recounted the story. 'What happened next?'

I could hear sounds from upstairs. 'I'll have to go,' I told Ruth. 'They'll be down soon and I don't want–'

Ruth gave a shriek. 'Tell me the rest quick, or I'll go mad.'

'Mr Russell made them shake hands,' I said. 'Then Greg asked if it would be okay for him to carry on visiting Bernie.'

'And what did Mr Russell say?'

'He looked sort of questioningly at Kev, and Kev shrugged. He didn't look too happy though,' I told her. 'And then Greg stammered out, "You probably haven't heard. My dad's been charged with drunken driving and dangerous driving. The case'll be heard next month."'

*   *   *

BERNIE

She watched them walking out of the room together. Their names still escaped her, but she knew now that the fair-haired boy was her brother, and the others were her friends.

It had been great to have them all round her bed, chatting and laughing, but she couldn't follow a lot of the conversation. She just kept a smile on her face so they wouldn't realise.

One of them, the girl who came most often and she knew was a special friend, had mentioned school and exams, and they had all groaned. Bernie tried to recall her own school. She could visualise the building, and sitting in class, but she couldn't remember the names of subjects, or the teachers, except the one who came to see her, or anything about her studies. It was scary. How was she ever going to get back to normal? What was normal?

She shifted uncomfortably in the armchair. Her shoulder and arm ached, and the bright lights in the ward hurt her eyes.

When she closed them, she saw again in her mind the reflection in the mirror of the ghastly-looking stranger with no hair, who turned out to be herself. And to think that when she'd seen the nurse with the long fair hair like her own, she hadn't realised that her own hair was gone. She started to laugh, and then to cry.

She felt a light touch. Someone was dabbing her face inexpertly with a tissue, drying the tears. She opened her eyes. It was him, the other fella, with the red hair. His nose looked red, swollen, as though he'd banged into something. 'What's up, Bernie?' he asked gently.

She shook her head. Just seeing him made her feel better. He always spoke softly and slowly so she could understand.

He showed her what was left of the flowers. She looked at him inquiringly.

'What ... happened?'

He grinned. 'I dropped them,' was all he said. 'I'll bring you fresh ones, tomorrow.'

She smiled. She knew he didn't mind how dreadful she looked, or about her hair. 'Thanks,' she whispered. He took her good hand and held it. She drifted into a doze.

He sat there for a long time, still holding her hand.

The Letter

'Jackie! Come down here this instant!' Mum's voice sounded frantic.

Now what? I wondered. I was juggling so many secrets that I knew something was bound to slip out eventually. Not yet though, I hoped. Not till after Kev's case the next day.

Grabbing my school raincoat I ran downstairs, keeping an eye on the time. They were always extra vigilant in school on Monday mornings.

But when I entered the kitchen I stopped short. Mum was sitting at the table in her dressing-gown in tears. The local newspaper lay open on the table. Dad, grim-faced, was standing by the window, holding a letter. Philip was pretending he wasn't there.

'Well, Jackie,' said Dad, his voice tight with suppressed anger. 'It seems there's a lot going on that you haven't seen fit to tell us about.'

My heart sank to my boots. Here we go, I thought. 'What d'you mean?' I knew I was starting on the wrong foot.

'What do I mean?' he repeated furiously. 'Don't pretend you don't know. Let's start with the letter from school.'

'From school?' I hadn't expected that. Dad waved the letter. 'It's from your class teacher, Miss Kinsella, and she wants to know if you are having problems at home.'

Problems at home? 'Why?' I asked, my stomach churning.

'You tell me,' said Dad. 'Apparently you've been inattentive, consistently late, you've missed homework deadlines, and on top of all that you were absent from school one morning without explanation.'

'And as if that wasn't bad enough,' Mum said tearfully, 'it says here in the paper that a boy from Ballytymon was up in court for malicious damage which he committed in revenge for an accident–'

'And it gives his name, Kevin Sinnott,' finished Dad.

'We were never happy about your relationship with that young man,' Mum said accusingly. 'But you knew better. You insisted we were prejudiced against him, because he came from Ballytymon.'

'And we were stupid enough to listen to you and accept him,' said Dad.

There was a silence. I was beginning to feel like a a suspect in 'NYPD Blue', being questioned by two tough cops. The sick feeling in my stomach started to turn to resentment.

'If you want to know why I didn't tell you about Kev,' I said slowly, 'it's because I knew you'd judge him without even listening to his side of the story. And that's what you've done, with me as well as with him.' I was amazed to hear myself sounding quite cool and calm, although in fact I was on the verge of tears.

Out of the corner of my eye I noticed Philip creeping out of the room. I didn't blame him. I just wished I could do the same.

Dad looked taken aback at my words. 'Look,' he said, sounding more normal, 'let's sit down and discuss this in a civilised manner. Though I don't see how anything you tell us can change the facts. It says he pleaded guilty, after all.'

'And this letter,' said Mum. 'How can you possibly justify mitching off school, for any reason?' She sniffed scornfully. 'And this nonsense about problems at home. What problems could you possibly have?'

Her words stabbed me. I felt something snap inside, and a huge torrent of misery and anxiety which had built up since the dreadful day of the accident swept through me like a flood.

I began to sob uncontrollably, loud rasping sobs that hurt my throat. I heard my voice, sounding high and strange, as though it belonged to someone else. 'How can you say I haven't got problems? Since Bernie's accident everything's gone wrong with my life as well as hers, and her mother's and Kev's.' I tried to force back the sobs. 'And do you know what the worst thing is?'

They were both on their feet now, and their angry expressions were turning to concern. But there was no stopping now. 'The worst thing's been the way I've had to cope with it all on my own,' I went on. 'Even when Bernie was so sick, you didn't really care–'

Mum started to say something, but Dad put a restraining

hand on her arm. 'Let her finish,' he said.

'–And when Kev got into trouble because he was so bitter about Bernie,' I continued, 'I knew there was no point in telling you because you wouldn't even listen to his side of the story. I knew you didn't care about him either, and his ma's sick, and he's got no-one except me–'

Dad came and put his arm round me, but I shook it off, and rushed into the hall. They both followed me. At the front door I turned and said, still sobbing, 'You think studying and exams are the only things that matter. Maybe they're important. But I happen to think people matter more than anything.'

And before they could answer, I ran out of the house, slamming the front door behind me. I dashed down the path, into the road and round the corner, blinded by tears.

I could hear them calling after me, but I didn't stop, though I had a sharp pain in my side from running, and I knew I must look a terrible mess.

I had no hesitation about where to go. I was going to the hospital, to Bernie.

The Change

'Just another step, dear,' said the young white-jacketed woman encouragingly to Bernie. 'That's it, you're doing great.'

Standing at the door of Ward B7 I watched as Bernie, leaning heavily on two walking sticks, took tiny faltering steps along the centre of the ward. The woman was holding her by the arm, and Mrs Sinnott was hovering behind them. To my relief there was no sign of the ward sister.

'Well done, Bernie,' called the woman in the opposite bed.

'Careful, love,' said Mrs Sinnott. 'Watch where you're going.'

'Now you're going to turn here very slowly,' said the woman steering Bernie. 'Put your weight on the left stick.'

Bernie turned obediently and saw me in the doorway. She smiled with delight, lifted the left stick an inch, and waggled it back and forth in greeting. Bad as I felt, I couldn't help smiling too.

'Jackie!' said Mrs Sinnott, 'this isn't your usual time.

Shouldn't you be in school?' As the slow procession came closer and she saw my tear-stained face, she added in a tone of concern, 'Are you all right, dear?'

I nodded, and she said nothing more.

'Hi,' said Bernie. She was wearing a long South Park T-shirt. I could see she was too preoccupied trying to think of my name to register the state of my face.

'Hi, Bernie, it's Jackie,' I said quickly.

'This is the ...' She paused.

'I'm the physio,' said the woman holding Bernie's arm. 'She's coming on great with the walking.'

The fair-haired nurse was straightening Bernie's bed. 'And her memory's definitely improving,' she said. 'She asked to see her sisters today, didn't you, Bernie?'

Bernie sank into the armchair beside the bed and sat breathing heavily, clearly drained by the effort of trying to walk.

'I'll leave you in peace, Bernie,' said the physio. 'Same time tomorrow.'

The nurse brought another chair and put it beside Bernie's. 'You sit with Bernie and have a chat,' Mrs Sinnott said to me. 'That does wonders for her. I'll be back in a few minutes.' We both watched her leave the ward.

'She's ... not ...' Bernie tried again. 'Not ... good.'

'She's better than she was,' I said. 'And she has Kev and your aunt and uncle.'

Bernie nodded. 'But ... it's hard .. . for her,' she managed. 'With me–' She broke off as a trolley was wheeled in and a nurse brought two cups of tea over to us. I held the cup for Bernie as she sipped the tea.

Then I picked up *Teen Dreams* magazine from beside the bed and scanned it to see if there was anything I could read out to her. I'd started doing that after I'd noticed her flicking through magazines and then putting them down without reading them. The doctor had told us that Bernie had difficulty concentrating.

'Read ...' Bernie stopped.

'The problem page?' To my relief she shook her head. Problems were the last thing I wanted to read about.

'Stars?' I asked. She nodded.

'You're Gemini aren't you? "*This month you need to redouble your efforts to achieve the goals you have set yourself,*"' I read. 'I suppose they mean walking with one stick instead of two.'

'Or remembering ... two peoples' names,' said Bernie, almost normally. We both giggled.

Then she looked up and frowned. I followed her glance. Two people were coming into the ward, deep in conversation. One was Bernie's mother.

And the other was my dad.

*　　　　*　　　　*

'Bernie, how are you feeling?' Dad asked her, as I recovered from my amazement.

'I'm much–' She couldn't finish the sentence. I could see the shock in his face as he took in her appearance and her hesitant speech. Had he even listened, I wondered, when I'd attempted to describe what had happened to Bernie? Or maybe you couldn't appreciate the extent of the damage till you saw her.

Mrs Sinnott came to the rescue. 'She's improving slowly,' she said. She didn't add, 'but there's a long way to go.' She didn't have to. After a moment Mrs Sinnott went on, 'I just want to tell you how good your daughter's been. She's a true friend to Bernie.'

Dad looked embarrassed. Bernie nodded agreement and took a deep breath. With an effort she said, 'Thanks ... Jackie.' We all burst into applause and her mother gave her a hug.

'That's the first time she's remembered my name,' I told Dad.

'I don't know what to say,' he said to Bernie's mother. 'I – we didn't realise–' He pulled himself together. 'Any news about the driver?' he asked her.

'Yes, the gardaí were on to me,' she said. 'He's been charged with drunken driving.'

'When will the case come up?' asked Dad.

'In a few weeks,' she replied. 'It's a slow business. I'm trying not to think about it.' In her voice I heard an echo of Kev's bitterness. 'The important thing is for Bernie to get well,' she continued. 'And, of course, we've got other problems.'

'I know,' said Dad. Mrs Sinnott threw a warning glance towards Bernie. Dad nodded and touched my shoulder. 'I'd better drive this young lady to school now, before she–' 'She gets into ... trouble,' put in Bernie unexpectedly. She grinned, and as we left she waved with her good hand.

*   *   *

In the car we were both silent. Then Dad said, 'Now I've seen Bernie, I can understand–' He broke off. Before I could speak he went on, 'You tried to tell us, I know. There was a failure on our part, and for that I'm sorry.'

'What about the letter from school?' I asked. 'And Kev's in court again tomorrow. I have to be there.'

To my surprise he said, 'I know.' I stared at him.

He handed me a note. 'I've explained why you're late this morning,' he said. 'And Mum and I are going to see Miss Kinsella to sort out everything out.'

I felt a kind of lightness, as though a burden had been lifted from me.

'Thanks, Dad,' I said, as we drew up outside the school gates. I got out of the car.

He stuck his head out of the window. 'And I'll be coming with you to court tomorrow,' he said. 'For moral support, for you both.' And he drove away.

*　　　　*　　　　*

We sat in the canteen at lunchtime that day munching crisps, except for Ruth, who was eating a muesli bar with a self-righteous air.

Though I hadn't said much, and they couldn't have known about the letter, the others seemed to understand that I wasn't feeling the best. No-one asked why I'd been late that morning, and everyone treated me with unaccustomed concern. They must have been discussing my problems and decided I needed what Ruth's favourite pop-group were called – TLC, which Deirdre the know-all had told us, wrongly as it turned out, meant Tender

Loving Care. Ruth even offered to get me a Galaxy bar, though we all knew she disapproved of them because of the high sugar content.

'Kev's case is tomorrow, isn't it?' asked Deirdre with a meaningful glance at the others. I nodded. 'Don't worry,' she went on. 'We'll say you had to go home sick or something.'

'No, it's okay,' I said. 'My dad's coming with me, so he'll tell Miss Kinsella.'

'Oh, I see.' Deirdre looked slightly put out.

'Thanks a million anyway,' I added.

'Er, Ruth and I are going in to see Bernie after school today,' said Therese.

'And I'm going tomorrow,' said Deirdre. 'So you needn't worry if the court thing runs on.'

They all watched my reaction. 'Great,' I said flatly.

I knew I ought to sound more pleased at all this sudden support. But I couldn't help feeling that they might have bothered more about Bernie all along, not just now when there was a crisis.

Anyway, I was so dazed and weary from the events of the day that I just didn't have the energy to be enthusiastic. And the relief I'd felt at Dad's change in attitude was becoming clouded over with worry about Kev's case.

I heaved a sigh, and they all gazed at me anxiously. I was beginning to feel suffocated by all this concern. Shrugging off my thoughts, I said to Deirdre, 'How's things with Mark?'

And to everyone's relief we resumed one of our normal discussions about Mark, Andy, Monika, fellas in general, and Deirdre's new jacket on which everyone had an envious eye.

The Trial

Sitting nervously beside Dad on the hard wooden bench in the court-house, I looked round at the blue-painted walls and the strange high arched windows. It felt a bit like being in a church, although the lawyer had told us the building used to be a school.

Kev was sitting in front of us beside his uncle. He was wearing his good jacket, and his hair was neatly combed. Even the stray lock that usually fell in his eyes was in place. I gazed at the back of his head, knowing that the sick feeling in my stomach was nothing compared to the way he must be feeling.

All round us there was a buzz of conversation. The place was crammed with people. There were several gardaí, all wearing navy sweaters which made them look somehow more approachable than their usual uniforms.

'Who are they all?' I whispered to Dad.

'I suppose they're a mix of offenders and their families, lawyers, social workers, court officials,' said Dad. 'You never realise all this is going on here every day, unless you're involved yourself.'

Even he sounded a bit subdued by the thought.

*   *   *

When we'd arrived the yard outside had been full of people standing in groups. Kev had looked taken aback at the sight of Dad and me. He obviously thought I was in some sort of trouble, because he cast an anxious glance at Dad and mumbled to me, 'You didn't need to come, I'll be okay.'

'We're here to give you some moral support,' announced Dad, to my embarrassment. He went on, 'How do you think it'll go?'

'We're hoping for a probation order,' said the lawyer.

When Kev had disappeared off to the loo, Dad asked the lawyer, 'What's the worst he could get?'

'Well, the judge could take a poor view of a deliberate decision to invade someone's home and cause damage, whatever the provocation,' he answered. 'There is some risk of a custodial sentence.' That meant prison, I guessed, judging by the faces of Dad and Kev's uncle. Fear stirred inside me.

'But surely there are special circumstances,' argued Dad. 'His situation at home, and his sister's accident.'

The lawyer nodded. 'Hopefully the judge'll be aware of all that from the probationer's report. But still–'

Kev's uncle shot him a warning look as Kev returned. Kev kept hugging himself as if he felt cold, even in his jacket. Catching my eye, he gave me a strained smile. I longed to put my arms round him and say something to soothe away some of the stress which was so obvious in his face. But with all these people around the best I could do was to stand very close to him. I could feel him shivering in the chill sunshine.

'It'll be okay,' I whispered to him as people started streaming towards the tiny doorway into the court room. 'They'll understand.' He gave a wan smile. If only I felt as confident as I sounded.

As we shuffled inside I thought of them all in school listening to Miss Kinsella droning on about J M Synge and Pegeen Mike and I wished I was safely back in the classroom instead of in this strange, threatening world of lawyers and social workers and probation orders, whatever they were.

*   *   *

'All rise.'

Everyone rose to their feet as the black-robed woman judge entered the court-room, gave a little nod, and seated herself in a big chair in front of the arched window. There was a long table nearby at which several men, some of them gardaí, sat scribbling notes.

The judge was wearing tinted glasses with heavy frames, and her hair was set in a style that reminded me of Nana's when she'd just got back from her hairdresser. But my heart sank as I registered her grim expression.

'The DPP against Kevin Sinnott,' announced a voice.

Kev leapt to his feet and went hurriedly to the front of the court, where his lawyer was waiting.

'What's the DPP?' I muttered to Dad.

'The Director of Prosecutions.'

Kev stood, a lonely figure, facing the judge.

'I'm appearing for Kevin Sinnott, Judge,' said the lawyer. 'I believe you have the probation officer's report before you.'

The judge leafed through papers on her desk and picked one out. 'Yes, I've read it.' My heart sank even further at the sharpness of her tone.

'Er, then you'll see, Judge, that there are special circumstances in this case.'

The judge continued to shuffle through her papers.

'You might find it useful to hear some of the circumstances—' continued the lawyer.

'They're in the report, aren't they?' snapped the judge.

But the lawyer ploughed on. 'The probation officer is in the court and could clarify some of the details.'

Eventually the judge nodded, and a young woman stood up. A man handed her a bible, and she said, 'I swear by Almighty God that the evidence I shall give in this case will be the truth, the whole truth, and nothing but the truth.'

Just like on TV, I thought. 'That must be Kathy,' I whispered to Dad. 'Kev says she's great.' I noticed she wasn't wearing the jeans today, but a navy suit with a short skirt.

'Er, you refer in the report to the defendant being very angry and upset as a result of his sister's accident,' said the judge. 'I take it you consider a period of probation would be helpful in this case?'

'I do, Judge,' said Kathy. 'As you say, it's understandable that he feels anger and concern about his sister. And of course, about his mother, who is not well enough to be present.' A memory flashed across my mind of Mrs Sinnott sitting by Bernie's bed, weeping soundlessly. 'But it's clear that he has dealt inappropriately with this anger,' Kathy went on. 'He recognises that he was wrong, and I found both him and his family most co-operative. I could certainly help him address some of his problems during a probation period.'

Kev's uncle turned round to us. 'That's sounds good,' he said.

'Yes,' agreed Dad. But they both wore worried frowns. I couldn't see Kev's face, but his back was rigid. I could imagine how he felt, standing there while they talked about him. I wished I was near him.

Beside me, Dad caught my eye and gave me an encouraging little smile. I tried to smile back, but my face felt stiff. Still, having Dad there made a difference. I must tell him afterwards, I thought.

*　　　　*　　　　*

Then the lawyer said, 'What do you have to say to the court and to the Gilmartin family's lawyer about this incident?' With a stab of alarm I realised he was addressing Kev.

There was a silence. Then Kev said hoarsely, 'I want to ... apologise for ... what I did. I was angry. I know it was the wrong way to–' He broke off. I looked down at my clenched hands. Let him find the right words, I begged silently.

'That's all very well, but how do I know the next time

you get angry that you won't do something like this again?' demanded the judge.

'N-no, it won't happen again,' said Kev. His voice shook.

The judge glared at him. 'This is a very serious matter,' she declared. 'I could send you to St Patrick's Institution for Young Offenders, and I'm tempted to do so.' She paused ominously. I held my breath. 'However,' she continued, 'I have taken into account what your lawyer, and the proba- tion officer have said. I have decided to put you on proba- tion for a period of one year.'

I let out my breath so loudly that Kev's uncle turned round. 'That means,' continued the judge, 'that you must do what the probation officer tells you, see her on a regular basis, be there when she visits your home, and co-operate with her in every way.'

Kev nodded. She went on sternly, 'If you don't abide by these conditions the officer will bring you back before this court, and I'll deal with you. Your behaviour was totally out of order. If you do anything that results in your coming back before me again, you won't be treated so leniently.' She sat back in her chair.

'Thank goodness for that,' Kev's uncle whispered to us. But the judge hadn't finished.

'Are you working? Earning money?' she asked Kev. He nodded, 'He's on a FÁS training course, Judge,' said the lawyer.

'How much do you estimate the damage, guard?' asked the judge.

The garda called out, 'I understand, Judge, that it would cost sixty pounds to replace the window.'

The judge said to Kev, 'You must pay the sixty pounds at your local garda station within three months.' That's not going to be easy for Kev, I thought. Maybe I could lend him some of the money I was saving for the fleece jacket. The judge dismissed Kev with a nod and he walked over to where Kathy, the probation officer, and the lawyer were waiting for him.

'If he hasn't got the money, I'll make him a small loan,' said Dad, to my surprise as we rose stiffly from our seats. 'That lad's had a hard time,' he went on. 'And his mother's got enough problems, without trying to find sixty pounds.'

'Thanks Dad,' I said. But I wondered if Kev would accept a loan from either of us, helpful though it might be.

I looked over at Kev, who was talking to Kathy. Then I heard the judge calling him back. 'Oh no,' I groaned to Dad. 'I thought it was over.'

'Don't forget to sign the probation bond before you leave court,' she said, her grim expression unchanged from the moment she'd entered.

*   *   *

It was still cold when we went outside, but never had the air seemed more fresh and crisp, or the autumn colours of the trees along the road more bright and cheering. Kev kept drawing deep breaths, as though he hadn't been able to breathe properly inside. There were tiny beads of sweat on his forehead.

The probation officer spoke to Kev's uncle. Then she said to Kev, 'How's your mother?'

'She's really worried,' he said. 'She wanted to come, but–'

'Well, at least you've some good news for her,' said Kathy. She glanced at me. 'Is this the sensible girlfriend?' Everyone laughed, and Dad added, 'And I'm the sensible girlfriend's father.'

The lawyer came and shook hands with Kev and his uncle and Dad. They all thanked him. As they chatted, Kev and I moved a few steps away.

'How d'you feel?' I asked him, glad to see that the lock of hair was back in his eyes.

'Better.' He gave a rueful grin. 'But I don't want to go through that again in a hurry.'

I gazed up at the brilliant blue sky. 'I wish we could go up the mountains for a long walk on our own,' I said to him.

'We will,' said Kev. 'Maybe this weekend.'

It was beginning to dawn on me that with Kev's case out of the way and with the new atmosphere at home, things were looking up at last. Maybe if Bernie got better, and the driver was punished, and I caught up with some study, Kev and I could start living normal lives again. I'd almost forgotten what normal life was.

The Halloween Disco

It was several weeks later.

Having spent hours getting ready for the school Halloween disco, I'd finally settled on a Nike T-shirt, hipsters borrowed from Ruth, black high heels and my new fleece jacket.

'Mum says I'm old enough to go with you to the disco,' said Philip as I descended the stairs. 'And I'm going to bring Mary Rose.'

I glared at him. The disco was going to be the first time the gang had got together since the traumatic events involving Bernie and Kev and all of us. To have Philip and Mary Rose tagging along would ruin everything.

'Now, Philip,' called Mum from the living room where she and Nana were watching TV. 'That's not what I told you. I said you'd be old enough in a year or two.'

'Get lost, Philip,' I said, relieved.

'Come in and let us see you dressed up, Jackie.' I went in reluctantly, knowing they were going to be disappointed.

Sure enough Nana said, 'I don't know why everything

they wear these days seems to be black or white. What's wrong with a bit of colour?' She turned to Mum. 'A nice pink frilly blouse would really set off that outfit.'

'She looks very nice,' said Mum, shooting her a look.

'Oh yes, very nice,' Nana agreed hastily.

'Those earrings look familiar,' said Mum. 'Have you worn them before?'

'They're yours,' I said. 'I got them out of that box in your drawer. I didn't think you'd mind.'

'Oh, I see,' said Mum. You could see her deciding not to make an issue of it.

'In my day–' began Nana.

Mum chimed in, 'Well, have a good time, dear.' She turned back to the TV, and after a moment, so did Nana. I tiptoed out of the room.

In the hall Dad was putting on his coat to give me a lift. 'Very nice,' he said when I emerged. 'Who are we collecting?'

'Just Deirdre and Ruth,' I told him. 'Therese'll probably be getting a lift, and Mark said he'd be late.'

'What about Kev?'

'He's coming with Andy.' And Monika no doubt, I thought. Apparently Andy never appeared anywhere without Monika now. Therese said Monika had done him the world of good. He was still a big head, but definitely not as cocky as he used to be.

*   *   *

In the car on the way to Deirdre's, Dad said, 'Did you know the case against Arthur Gilmartin was on yesterday?'

I stared at him. 'I thought it was next week.'

I couldn't believe I hadn't heard about it. But I'd been so busy catching up at school, and Kev with his FÁS training course, that we hadn't seen each other for a while. I hadn't even had a chance to hear how Bernie was since her recent return home from the rehab centre.

'How did you hear? I asked Dad.

'Kev's lawyer was in court. I'd asked him to keep me posted about it,' he said. 'I gather Gilmartin was convicted of drunken driving *and* dangerous driving,'

'I'm glad he was convicted,' I said. 'What did he get?'

'He was sentenced to twelve months imprisonment. But the judge said in view of the fact that it was a first offence—'

'A first offence?' I interrupted. 'His son said he's had a drink problem for years.'

'That may be,' said Dad. 'But this is his first conviction for dangerous driving. Anyway, instead of prison, he's to do 240 hours of community service.'

'What does that mean?' I asked.

'Cleaning up graveyards, painting and decorating old folks centres, that sort of thing,' said Dad. 'The lawyer said the judge told Gilmartin that he'd caused serious injury to a young girl, and great distress to her family, and he said Gilmartin had to agree to go for proper treatment for his drink problem. He was fined five hundred pounds. And he's disqualified from driving for five years.'

'Five years?'

'Yes. I think that's the maximum,' said Dad. 'That could

make life very difficult for him.'

'I hope so,' I said sharply. 'Look what he did to Bernie's life. But Kev'll be raging. He thought Gilmartin should be sent to prison.'

'He has a point. But it wouldn't help Bernie,' said Dad, as the car turned into Ruth's road. 'There are all kinds of punishments. Apart from anything else, Gilmartin has to live with knowing what his drinking and driving did to Bernie. And hopefully, the Sinnotts will take him to court to get compensation, and that could cost him plenty.'

Into my mind came a fleeting memory of Greg in the hospital clutching the bouquet of flowers for Bernie. I couldn't help thinking how hard all this was going to be on him and the rest of his family.

As we drew up outside Ruth's I said to Dad, 'Don't say anything about the case to the others, till I've had a chance to talk to Kev and see if he's heard.'

'I think the probation officer will have told him,' said Dad. 'But I'll say nothing. Anyway,' he added with a grin, 'you're supposed to be having a fun night at the disco after all that studying.'

'I sure hope so,' I said. But would it be a fun night? I wondered.

We picked up Ruth, who was wearing a white mini skirt and a tight black top, and Deirdre, in black Levi's and a black bodywarmer.

Good thing Nana didn't see them, I thought. Not a pink frilly blouse in sight.

*   *   *

The first person I saw in the school hall, decorated for the disco with paper lanterns and balloons, was Monika, dressed to kill in a quilted waistcoat with silver buttons and a black velvet hat. I nudged Deirdre as Monika came rushing over, with Andy following behind.

'Jackie, it is so good to see you!' she said, waving her hands, which were laden with rings. She turned to Deirdre. 'You are Deirdre, I think,' she said. 'I hear many nice things from Andy concerning you.'

'I bet,' said Deirdre.

Andy quickly changed the subject. 'Anyone hear how the dangerous driving case is going?' If he knew it was on, then Kev probably did, I thought anxiously. But I said nothing.

'It was supposed to start yesterday,' said Ruth.

'These sort of cases could take a few days,' said Deirdre. 'Anyway, wouldn't Kev have been there?'

I had been scanning the room for Kev. 'Didn't he come with you?' I asked Andy.

'No,' he said. 'I haven't seen him.'

A wave of disappointment washed over me. This was the first school disco Kev had planned to come to, and I'd been counting the days. And now he wasn't here. Could it be because of the case? Maybe he was freaked out about the result, and had gone off the rails again. I didn't dare think about the possible consequences of that.

'How is the girl who was injured by the car?' asked Monika.

'She's been in the rehab centre,' said Ruth. 'So none of us have seen her for a while.' And Kev might have let me know how Bernie was too, I thought resentfully.

I tried to suppress these seething thoughts. I'd promised myself I was going to relax and enjoy the disco. I forced myself to switch back to the conversation.

'Is Therese here?' Monika was asking. 'She was so kind, Jackie, on that first day I came to Ballytymon to find Andy.'

'Was she?' I said doubtfully. 'Therese?'

'Oh yes,' said Monika. 'I remember she said how both of you must come with me and Kevin to Andy's house, to make sure I will find him.' She fluttered her mascara'd eyelashes. 'Was that not kind, Andy?'

'Oh yeah,' said Andy wryly.

'Therese'll probably be here soon,' I told her. 'How do you like Ireland, Monika?'

'It is, how you say, cool,' she said eagerly. 'I am improving much my English, and soon Andy is going to introduce to me his friends The Corrs!'

'Is he really?' said Deirdre, giggling. 'I didn't know you knew them, Andy.'

He grinned sheepishly. 'Er, I know someone whose cousin went to school with a brother of one of them.'

'We'd all like to meet them, Andy,' I said wickedly. 'Maybe you can have them over to your place some time and we'll all come.'

Monika gave a little shriek. 'A party! That will be *wunderbar!*'

'Yeah,' said Deirdre mockingly. 'It'd be *wunderbar,* all right.'

*   *   *

An hour later the music was blaring and everyone was dancing, but there was still no sign of Kev. I made myself chat and laugh with the others, but inside I felt a hard knot of misery. Why hadn't he come? Everything that had happened during the last turbulent weeks had seemed to bring Kev and me closer than ever before. And yet, I thought sadly, I still couldn't depend on him.

'Not dancing, Jackie?' Miss Kinsella was addressing me with a frosty smile.

'Er, just having a break,' I answered, as we watched Monika flinging herself about in an over-the-top sort of way opposite an embarrassed-looking Andy.

Miss Kinsella lowered her voice. 'I was sorry to hear about your friend's accident. I hope she's improving now?' I nodded.

'It must be difficult for the family,' she said kindly. I said nothing. Although I knew she meant well, the last thing I felt like doing was launching into the whole story again.

Our attention was distracted by a commotion at the entrance to the hall. I could hear Ruth's unmistakable shriek.

'What's going on over there?' Miss Kinsella's tone resumed its normal sharpness. She strode to the door to see what the fuss was about. Following in her wake, I heard Ruth calling me. I quickened my step.

A slow-moving little group had come in through the swing doors. My heart gave an enormous lurch when I realised who it was.

Kev, in his black jacket, his hair flopping in his eyes as

he looked round, searching, I hoped, for me. Therese, wearing a new Calvin Klein shirt.

And between them, walking very slowly with a stick, her face still thin and pale but lit up with a valiant smile, was Bernie.

The Reconciliation

'Sorry I couldn't ring,' said Kev, as Bernie, at the centre of a chattering group, seated herself slowly and carefully on the chair that Ruth had hurriedly brought over.

'It's okay.' My sadness and resentment had melted away as soon as I'd laid eyes on Kev, and grasped the fact of Bernie's presence.

'Jackie,' said Bernie, reaching out her hand to me. I could feel instantly how much stronger her grip was now.

'You look great,' I said to her. And she did, wearing her familiar Levi's and a silk blouse, the bruises almost entirely gone from her face, her short fair hair curling softly all over her head. 'How was the rehab place?'

She grimaced. 'It was ... hard work,' she said. 'But ... I got a lot ... of help.' Although she still spoke hesitantly, it was clear that the words came to her more easily. She went on, 'How's ... everything?'

'Fine,' I said, deciding this wasn't the time to tell her how things had really been. I wondered if she'd been told about Kev's attack on Gilmartin, or about the dangerous driving case. Better not say anything, I thought, until I could find out how much she knew, and how much she could handle.

She looked over at Monika. 'Who's that?' she asked me. I started to explain about Monika and Andy, and about Deirdre being back with Mark.

Then Miss Kinsella came up to us and welcomed Bernie. The others were dancing. Kev stood by silently. I noticed he never moved too far from Bernie. I was desperate to talk to him about the Gilmartin case, but I couldn't while Bernie was in earshot.

Catching Therese's eye I decided it was time for some assertiveness. I whispered to her, 'Keep your eye on Bernie for a bit. I want to talk to Kev.'

She nodded, and I went up to Kev. 'Let's dance.'

He glanced over at Bernie. She'd obviously heard me, because she said, 'Go on. I'll be fine.'

Kev looked down at me. Why was he so calm? Maybe he hadn't heard.

'Sure,' he said.

* * *

When we'd been dancing for a bit, and just as I was wondering what to say, Kev said, 'That case was on today.' At last, I thought. Aloud I said, 'Were you there?'

He pulled me away from the dance floor and I followed him out of the hall.

'None of us went,' he said, when we were outside. 'We've had enough of courts. Kathy came for a visit today, and she told us what happened. But we were all up to our eyes helping Bernie get ready for tonight, so I didn't get a chance to give you a call.'

My heart felt lighter as I listened to him. 'My dad heard,' I said. 'He told me.' After a moment I asked nervously, 'What d'you think about the result?'

Kev shrugged. 'I think he should have gone to prison, and so does everyone else,' he said. 'But Kathy told us Gilmartin was shattered when he heard about losing his licence for five years. His lawyer'd told the judge that his work depended on him having a driving licence, so he'll probably lose his job.'

That was something I hadn't thought of. All in all, there were going to be a lot of problems ahead for Gilmartin. And his family.

Kev went on, his grey eyes fixed on mine, 'Jackie, my ma says that this way, every day that Gilmartin has to manage without being able to drive, especially if he's lost his job, he'll be reminded of what he did to Bernie.' He swallowed hard. Then he added. 'And it'll be prison for him if he ever does this again to anyone else.'

There was a silence. 'So he didn't get off scot-free in the end,' I said.

'No,' Kev admitted. He grinned. 'Kathy pointed that out to me too.'

'How's Bernie now?' I asked him.

Kev put his arm around me and the old warm glow stole over me. So it was still there, I thought. 'She's much better,' he said. 'But there's a lot she doesn't remember. And I never told her about what I did at the Gilmartin's house that night.'

'Didn't Greg ever tell her?' I asked him.

'I don't think so,' he said. 'She doesn't seem to know.' He drew me closer, so that I could feel his heart beating. 'I don't feel so bad about it all now,' he went on. 'I'll always hate Arthur Gilmartin. But my ma said that if I go on being bitter and letting him wreck my life, he'll have messed up the lives of two of our family instead of one.'

I'd never heard Kev talk like this. He seemed almost like a different person, as though he'd grown up in some way.

That was my last rational thought as he bent down to kiss me. As his lips touched mine, my body was filled with a powerful sensation of warmth and softness, shot through with a kind of sharp excitement. Everything else vanished from my mind.

*   *   *

When we went back inside, Kev's arm around me, I was still enveloped by the soft cloud. We walked over to the others. Mark had arrived, and was just going to dance with Deirdre. He looked uneasy, I thought.

Bernie was still sitting in the centre of the group. She looked flushed and happy, her eyes shining. Someone was bending down to talk to her.

Kev stopped, and withdrew his arm. I felt suddenly chilled.

'I don't believe it,' he said angrily. 'It's Greg Gilmartin.'

*   *   *

BERNIE

It was wonderful to be at the disco with all her friends, like in the old days, before the accident. It was worth the weeks in the rehab centre, the hours of exercises with the physio, the endless speech practice, the homesickness she had felt, even though the people there were so kind and patient and gave her such devoted care and encouragement.

She still got headaches, the muscles of her arm and shoulder were weak, and it hurt to eat or yawn, or even to cough. Speaking was still an effort, and she tired easily.

She could remember a great deal more now. But there was still so much she didn't understand, and huge gaps. She had no memory of the accident, and only a hazy recollection of the weeks of pain and distress that had followed.

She had to depend on her mother and Kev for a lot of things now, rather than the other way round. Her little sisters were glad to have her home, but they seemed to look on her as an affectionate stranger rather than their familiar big sister.

Although everyone told her that in time she would be back the way she'd been before, she had a haunting suspicion that she was never going to be the same person again.

Bernie was aware that the people who had helped her most through her ordeal, apart from the doctors and nurses and physios, were her ma, her brother Kev, her friend Jackie, her teacher, and the mysterious fella with red hair, who used to come so often when she was in the hospital. She couldn't remember his name, but she often dreamed about him.

'You'll be able for dancing yourself soon,' Therese shouted to her above the loud disco music. She nodded in reply, but she was starting to feel tired, and her head throbbed. She tried to spot Kev and Jackie, but there was no sign of them.

'Bernie?' said a voice she remembered. He was standing close to her, the fella with the red hair. 'I found out from Mark you might be here,' he told her softly. 'He's in my class in school. D'you remember me from the hospital? Greg Gilmartin?'

She nodded, delight bubbling up inside her.

'I wanted to explain something to you,' he stammered.

'I remember ... the flowers and the perfume,' said Bernie. She felt a surge of joy at seeing him again, this time not in a dream. She remembered him sitting by her bed, holding her hand.

But she could see that his freckled face was anxious. She waited. Then he said in a rush. 'I have to tell you ... the driver who knocked you down. He's my father.'

Bernie understood. A shock went through her. For a moment she said nothing. Kev and Jackie appeared, and she saw Kev's face change, becoming tense at the sight of Greg. It was clear to her that Kev knew who he was.

Bernie suddenly felt terribly tired. But she knew she had to speak. To explain that what Greg had just told her didn't change the way she felt about him. Summoning all her strength she said clearly, 'Greg ... It wasn't your fault.'

Kev made a movement. Bernie's eyes met his. Could he, would he understand?

For a few seconds no-one spoke.

Bernie saw Jackie take Kev's hand. Then Kev shrugged, and gave a nod, and the tension in his body relaxed, as though in acceptance. Beside her, Greg gave a little sigh.

Then her friend Jackie came close and touched her. 'I know you're tired, Bernie,' she said. 'But doesn't it feel good to be back, with all of us?' As she spoke, Jackie looked round the silent circle of people, deliberately including Greg in her glance.

Bernie gave a tired smile. 'It's magic,' she said.

THE JACKIE AND KEV TRILOGY
from Marilyn Taylor

COULD THIS BE LOVE?
I WONDERED

It begins with a look: but when Jackie actually meets the boy from the bus stop, it's not so simple. Is Kev interested in her or not? Her friends are full of advice, but how can she tell for sure?

Romance isn't the only challenge for Jackie. At home there are money problems and her young brother's brush with the law. Why is life so easy in films and so complicated in real life, she wonders.   Paperback £4.99

COULD I LOVE A STRANGER?

Daniel, a dark mysterious boy, comes to stay – when Jackie's boyfriend Kev, is working abroad. Why is Jackie so attracted to Daniel? Is it simply the diary he shares with her, which documents the heart rending story of a Jewish family in Nazi Germany and their attempts to escape to freedom?

Jackie has to make some difficult choices involving Daniel, Kev and her best friend, Deirdre. A dramatic event on a beach brings the conflict to a head.   Paperback £4.99

Other Books from The O'Brien Press

ALLISON
Tatiana Strelkoff

When Karen meets Allison her world is turned upside down. What are these feelings she has for this girl? Can she trust her own heart? There is danger in being different. Can Karen overcome peer prejudice, parental opposition and the very real threat to her life from the school bully to remain true to herself and find happiness?

Paperback £5.99

SISTERS...NO WAY!
Siobhán Parkinson

Cindy does NOT want her Dad to remarry after her mother's death – especially not Ashling's mum. No way do these two want to become sisters! A flipper book, this story comprises the very different diaries of the two girls as they try to come to terms with the events unfolding in their lives.

Paperback £4.99

FRIEND OF MY HEART
Judith Clarke

Daz is in love with Valentine O'Leary, the biggest pig in Mimosa High School. Her brother William is in love with a girl he's never spoken to. Eleanor Wand, the music teacher, is in love with the headmaster. Everyone is in love with someone – and doing rather badly. Meanwhile, Daz's granny is searching for Bonnie, the long-ago friend of her heart. Will *anyone* be successful in the quest for lost friends and true love?

Paperback £3.99

THE HEROIC LIFE OF AL CAPSELLA

Judith Clarke

Al Capsella wants to be cool, to fit in with the other teenagers in his neighbourhood. And part of fitting in is to be like all the others – to be 'normal'. But despite his heroic efforts, Al faces a crippling pair of obstacles: his PARENTS. Along with schoolmates like Louis, Al has his own plans for surviving the abnormal and embarrassing antics of parents, grandparents and teachers.

Paperback £3.99

AL CAPSELLA AND THE WATCHDOGS

Judith Clarke

Al is now sixteen and faces a new set of challenges – a gang of prowling mothers who stalk the suburbs ever alert to his antics! Not only that, there's the unwelcome attentions of Sophie Disher, and a father whose interest in homework borders on the unhealthy.

Paperback £3.99

Send for our full colour catalogue